DOT.

R O B O T

Jason Bradbury likes gadgets – a lot! He has scoured the globe to find them and rarely stops talking and writing about them. He also likes computer games – perhaps even loves them. The first computer game he ever played consisted of nothing more than two dots and a straight line, but it was enough to ignite a lifelong passion for the (pixellated) pastime – and, despite having two children and a robot called Vernon to look after, Jason still finds time for more game playing than is wise.

He is best known as the host of Five's *The Gadget Show*, on which he swims with sharks, rides rocket-powered bicycles and jumps off bridges – but before his TV career took off he was a comedian, a script writer and a breakdancer.

Jason lives in London, where he cruises the streets on various electric vehicles and newfangled types of skateboard.

The science and technology in *Dot.Robot* is real and Jason has witnessed much of it first hand – including a trip in a self-driving robotic car in Las Vegas and a look at an invisible jacket . . . if you can look at something that's *invisible*.

To find out what Jason is up to, go to his website *jasonbradbury.com*

Books by Jason Bradbury

Dot.Robot

JASON BRADBURY

DOT.

ROBOT

PUFFIN

PUFFIN BOOKS

Published by the Penguin Group
Penguin Books Ltd, 80 Strand, London WC2R 0RL, England
Penguin Group (USA) Inc., 375 Hudson Street, New York, New York 10014, USA
Penguin Group (Canada), 90 Eglinton Avenue East, Suite 700, Toronto, Ontario, Canada M4P 2Y3
(a division of Pearson Penguin Canada Inc.)
Penguin Ireland, 25 St Stephen's Green, Dublin 2, Ireland (a division of Penguin Books Ltd)
Penguin Group (Australia), 250 Camberwell Road, Camberwell, Victoria 3124, Australia
(a division of Pearson Australia Group Pty Ltd)
Penguin Books India Pvt Ltd, 11 Community Centre, Panchsheel Park, New Delhi – 110 017, India
Penguin Group (NZ), 67 Apollo Drive, Rosedale, North Shore 0632, New Zealand
(a division of Pearson New Zealand Ltd)
Penguin Books (South Africa) (Pty) Ltd, 24 Sturdee Avenue, Rosebank, Johannesburg 2196,
South Africa

Penguin Books Ltd, Registered Offices: 80 Strand, London WC2R 0RL, England

puffinbooks.com

First published 2009
1

Set in Absara OT Light by Palimpsest Book Production Limited, Grangemouth, Stirlingshire
Made and printed in England by Clays Ltd, St Ives plc

British Library Cataloguing in Publication Data
A CIP catalogue record for this book is available from the British Library

ISBN: 978-0-141-32395-4

www.greenpenguin.co.uk

For Luther Francis Bradbury,
who told the best stories

CHAPTER 1

'Do you know any secrets?'

He almost didn't notice it. He was busy pulling himself on to a rocky crag high above the vale of Borelock, when the peculiar question blinked its way into Jackson's little corner of cyberspace. That was one of the problems with instant-messaging software – anyone could find you; anyone could make contact. You had to be careful. Dad never stopped reminding him of the fact. Jackson sighed. His dad didn't half go on sometimes.

'Who are you?' typed Jackson, his fingertips bouncing over the keys with the nimbleness of a tiny dancing troop.

'Do you know any secrets?' came the reply.

OK, so someone really didn't know when to back off and Jackson wasn't about to be made a fool of. In school, maybe. Perhaps after school, on the way home. There was little he could do about that. Jackson flinched at the thought. But not here, not in his domain.

He moved his cursor over the miniature silhouette

of his uninvited guest. A label materialized on the right-hand side, containing the words 'Elan Drivel'.

'Elan Drivel?' Jackson laughed out loud. What kind of a name was that?

There were stupid Messenger nicknames: 'MyDogBeatsMeUp' was one in Jackson's contact list. 'I'm-a-freak-don't-talk-to-me' was another, which he knew belonged to Amisha Patel, the Indian goth girl from Year 11. But none of those were as naff as using your real name. No one used their real name for Messenger.

Jackson was 'WizardZombie'. It was just about the coolest tag he'd come across. Think about it: a zombie was scary enough. But imagine a gang of undead sorcerers roaming your local shopping centre; now that was terrifying. It was a name that garnered respect – respect that was well deserved – as WizardZombie ruled *Whisper*, one of the most popular online role-playing games on the Web. If you knew *Whisper*, you knew WizardZombie.

This Drivel was obviously a 'n00bie', a novice, a lamer just asking to be blocked.

Jackson typed a countdown into the Messenger text bar, followed by his favourite atom-bomb emotion: '5, 4, 3, 2, 1, ==@'. Then, with a click of the BLOCK command, the stranger was gone.

Jackson turned back to the situation unfolding in the gorge below WizardZombie. Six trolls had surrounded two halflings. Trolls were vile creatures and Jackson had no idea why anyone would pay to spend their evenings playing as the stunted savages. It was an unfair match against the weaker halflings, and they knew it. They were playing with the halflings, like a cat plays with a mouse or a vole.

WizardZombie was a human, a human with more spells than any other he'd encountered. The question was which weapon from his arsenal of black artistry should he summon? Given the odds, a lesser player would choose an explosion, a giant spider spell or a plague of locusts; they'd go for the fireworks, something with bells and whistles. But not WizardZombie.

First he took stock of the surroundings. The troll raiders were in the middle of a deep gully. In front of them were the wide, open plains that led to the Gulliper trading post. Behind them, a steep, narrow path snaked its way through the Delvian mountain range and out to the coast.

WizardZombie selected a sandstorm from his inventory and, pointing towards the entrance to the gorge, fired it at the ground. The six fiends were instantly consumed in a gritty whirlwind.

There was only one way to go if they were to escape the blinding twister. Scrabbling over one another, they darted up the narrow mountain pass.

The fleeing mob didn't notice the first of their number to hit the ground. The second troll took an arrow in the forehead. They noticed that. Within moments they were counter-attacking, crossbow bolts flying up from the gorge with startling accuracy. But WizardZombie stood his ground. There were only four of them now and, with his agility, his trusty longbow should suffice.

'Do you know any secrets?' The message appeared again, brazenly, in the centre of his screen.

Jackson drew a sharp intake of breath. Before it had been mildly irritating; this time it was potentially fatal. Who? How? There wasn't time for questions. He punched in a key combination to block the pestilent visitor. The message disappeared for a split second and then rematerialized: 'Do you know any secrets?'

Jackson needed to act swiftly, or WizardZombie would be troll-bait. Hitting ALT and TAB, the Messenger box was exchanged for the game screen, as the third crossbow bolt penetrated WizardZombie's chest plate. Fireworks it was then.

WizardZombie's lightning strike hit the ravine floor with such force it cracked the rock face, vaporizing the four trolls and the two halflings instantaneously.

If he was to make it back to town and find a healer, WizardZombie would need to set up camp and rest. He lit a fire and settled down for the night. Jackson pressed ESC.

'It's a school night, son. Now I know that you're safely tucked up in bed and your computer is already off, but all the same, I'll check on my way back from the loo.' The warning came from behind Jackson's closed bedroom door, and it signalled two minutes before lockdown. Jackson only vaguely registered his dad's words as he sat fuming about Elan Drivel's intrusion.

It was puzzling that this uninvited ignoramus had managed to get a message through at all. New Messenger contacts couldn't just announce themselves on your screen. It was a feature of the software that they needed the user's permission first. So how had this Drivel character managed it? And then there was the question of the botched block. Jackson knew exactly how the blocking function worked: it logged a visitor's unique Internet ID number. Once that number was outlawed, the person associated with it was history. So how come Elan Drivel had repeatedly managed to get that dim-witted question on to Jackson's monitor?

The answer hit Jackson like one of WizardZombie's lightning strikes. Elan Drivel wasn't a person at all – it was a virus!

Jackson glanced at his bedside clock.

Thirty seconds.

Thirty seconds to prove his theory. *Damn it*, he thought. *There are high-security prison wardens who are more relaxed about lights out than my dad.*

Jackson was already into the settings for his Internet security software. He scrolled down the screen:

```
Intrusion Detection: On
Firewall Setting: High
Anti Virus: Medium
```

Medium? That must be it!

He looked at the clock.

Five seconds.

Wielding his mouse with samurai precision, Jackson was four layers deep into the program in a blink. At last the SYSTEM SCAN box appeared. At its centre was a bright red button surrounded by yellow-and-black hazard warning stripes and the words SCAN AND KILL written in the middle. He loved that: 'Scan and Kill'. It was so final.

One second.

Jackson hit the button, simultaneously stabbing the power switch on his monitor, leaving his computer to purr away stealthily under the desk.

When the crack of light appeared at the edge of the bedroom door, all was calm in Jackson HQ.

'Night, son,' said his father.

'Night, Dad,' replied Jackson.

CHAPTER 2

His pillow began to vibrate at around 3 a.m.

Jackson lifted the handset from under it, switched off the phone's alarm and used its indigo screen as a flashlight. Skimming the room with its beam, he located the desk by the glint of the trophies lined up proudly on the shelf above his monitor. They were ranked by order of importance from left to right: Buffy statuette, a light-seeking robot he'd sweated blood to build from plans on the Internet using an old mouse and some slot-car motors, a limited edition *Dr Who* Sonic Screwdriver won on eBay, the weightier and considerably more realistic replica of Yoda's light-sabre, and the pride of the fleet, the county chess prize. The blue glow from the phone screen was powerful enough to project the words FIRST PLACE through its tall perspex body and on to the wall behind. It was a title that was hard won. Not the chess final – Jackson had taken that in his stride – but the fallout. Victory's aftermath had been tough, with the announcement in assembly and the unwanted attention from Tyler Hughes and his gang. Jackson knew the script: 'They're just jealous.' 'They feel threatened by you cos you're clever.' 'You'll see, they'll all end up with ASBOs.' But friendly advice doesn't help when you're in a headlock and someone is jumping up and down on your iPod.

Jackson stumbled to his monitor and watched as it swapped his reflection for the vivid glare of his desktop. In the centre of his screen was the SYSTEM SCAN window he had left to do his bidding earlier. He inspected the results.

```
You were last attacked on:
    NEVER
Recent intrusion attempts:
    NONE
Recent viruses blocked: NONE
```

None? Never? No trace of anything? Jackson brooded. How could it be? His anti-virus program was bullet-proof; it couldn't have missed an infection like this.

If his own high-security settings couldn't stop this virus masquerading as a message, if it could slip un-detected past the best anti-virus software available, then what could Jackson do? If this was another sort of puzzle or an especially testing mission in *Whisper*, he'd have turned to the Web for help, checked out some forums, surfed a message board or two.

Jackson fired up his Internet browser. He didn't even wait for the graphics to load before entering 'Elan Drivel' and hitting SEARCH. A heartbeat later, tens of thousands of web links unravelled down the screen. A free list of Irish baby names. 'Feel like your kids talk meaningless drivel? Enrol in Parenting Classes.' 'Buy *A Guide to Dublin* and get an Irish dancing video absolutely free!' 'Try our online Anagram Machine.' Line after line of completely unhelpful suggestions. But no mention of a virus. Not by this name anyway.

Maybe he was searching for the wrong thing. What else was there? There was that question. Over and over again, that question that had breached every defence he had and buried itself in his head: 'Do you know any secrets?'

Jackson entered the sentence and groaned. Once again he was greeted by page after page of unhelpful links. An advert for a new chocolate bar: 'It's so good, you'll want to keep it to yourself.' 'My cat was abducted by a secret alien society.' *Poor cat!* thought Jackson.

Then, just as he was about to logoff and concede defeat, on page twelve of a possible 122,600 results something caught Jackson's eye.

doyouknowanysecrets•com

As websites went it was uncomplicated. No pictures. No colourful animations. The question at the top of the page, DO YOU KNOW ANY SECRETS?, followed by a smaller headline, WELL, DO YOU?

Jackson did know some secrets. He knew that his dad kept a secret stash of cigarettes in the garage for when he got really stressed. He knew a password for the school's computer server and what his teachers had said about him on his internal report form. It was quite complimentary, so he hadn't changed it. He knew that Marie Cohan was double-dating Tyler Hughes and that Hughes was only one formal warning away from expulsion. He knew a cheat for unlimited bowstaffs in *Whisper* and a way of downloading just about any TV show and movie he wanted for free. He knew lots of secrets and apparently he wasn't alone. Towards the bottom of the page were literally hundreds of secrets submitted by visitors to the site. 'The Father Christmas in my local DIY store isn't the real one. He is an actor paid by the store manager.' – posted by FatBarry. 'I pick my nose then shake hands with the boss. It makes me feel better.' – by Wonder Girl.

What was this? What was Jackson doing, sitting here at three in the morning? He wasn't sure this website had anything to do with the message that had kicked off this whole charade. He wasn't even sure if sharing a secret was right anyway – was a secret still a secret once you'd shared it? How many people could you tell?

What was the critical mass of a secret, the point at which it exploded into common knowledge? Now that was a mathematical problem that made even Jackson's head hurt. That or his lack of sleep.

He continued down the unending column of confessions, his mouse wheel beginning to feel heavy. That was until one entry stopped him in his tracks. A single sentence, in light grey text, barely a few millimetres high, followed by the name of the author, Elan Drivel:

```
I keep a secret stash of
       Easter eggs.
```

To most visitors, the secret would seem unremarkable, the innocent confession of a chocoholic. But for Jackson it held a whole other significance. He knew he wasn't going mad for starters. It was clear that someone, this Elan perhaps, had intended him to find his way to this site. And there was something about the secret that Jackson couldn't fail to notice, something that any self-respecting geek would immediately comprehend. 'Easter eggs' weren't just chocolate treats. The phrase also referred to hidden messages, undocumented features and secret back doors left in the code behind certain games, websites and even DVDs by their programmers. Jackson had been led to this site and now the mysterious messenger was telling him it had a secret entrance.

There was the dancing stormtrooper hidden in the DVD menu of the *Star Wars* box set if you knew which remote-control key combination to press. Jackson had even found a sign in a cave in *Whisper* that he suspected had been left by one of the game's developers. 'Hello, Mum' read the message, sprayed on the cave wall in a part of the game where only Elvish was spoken. Easter-egg hunting was all about being methodical. Nevertheless, having probed every link on the page, sifted every name for a nuance, even opened the VIEW SOURCE window to pour over the site's raw code, Jackson was out of ideas.

Then he saw it. As he was dragging his mouse pointer doggedly down the page, it momentarily switched to a hand. It happened so quickly Jackson wasn't sure if he'd imagined it. He tested the section of black background again, combing the area with his mouse arrow like a miniature minesweeper, hoping to see the angular pointer morph into the little hand again. But nothing happened. He was dog-tired. He felt like he'd been headbanging this puzzle all night and would have put the whole thing down to exhaustion were it not for a single grey pixel that blinked at him as he started to scroll down again.

The microscopic grey dot looked like a speck of dust on his monitor: barely a pixel in size. He had to lean closer and blink to keep it in vision. But sure enough, as he moved his mouse pointer back up the screen, this time placing it carefully over the dot, it suddenly changed into a tiny hand, an outstretched index finger confirming the presence of a live link.

It was now 4 a.m. or thereabouts and outside his window the birds were declaring their governance of the early morning, before the violent coup of the first of the traffic. Jackson should have been dead on his feet, but as he clicked the mouse button a second window popped up, black except for a luminous green text cursor winking in the top left. For the bleary-eyed Jackson this was caffeine.

After a few seconds of frustrating nothing, suddenly the cursor started to move, racing across the screen from left to right, leaving four lines of text in its wake.

```
>: Congratulations, Jackson.
Welcome to MeX.
You will be contacted again
    soon.
Goodbye.
```

There was a faint throb from under Jackson's desk, which he suspected was his hard drive, and a moment later his computer closed down.

Jackson stared at the empty screen, a dry patch forming in the back of his throat.

● CHAPTER 3

The Hummer H3R sports utility vehicle hurtled down the stony path at almost 80 kilometres per hour. Brooke English clung nervously to the armrest of the passenger seat, head down, laptop bouncing off her knees. No one was driving.

'Ow!' she yelped. 'Goddamit!' as her ruggedized metal laptop landed square on her kneecap for what felt like the thousandth time. The vehicle was driving itself, but in spite of the bank of four multi-core processors that filled the back seat and enough hardware on the roof to keep a space program happy, it seemed intent on changing the route at every opportunity. Brooke had built several automated robots before, but she'd never tested one by riding shotgun.

'Mom!' she yelled, trying to keep hold of her laptop with one hand, a rubber two-way radio in the other.

'Yes, darlin',' came her mother's calm reply.

'Where did you say the canyon was?' yelled Brooke.

'That'll be north-west, honey . . . don't go north-west.'

'Then we might have a bit of a problem,' replied Brooke in a voice that she hoped veiled genuine panic. She stared at the full-colour readout from the Global Positioning System receiver she had Velcroed on to the dashboard. In big letters it read '300 DEGREES. NORTH-WEST.'

Brooke and her mother had been working on the 'X Car Challenge' for the last six months. The aim of the extreme engineering competition was simple: design and build a vehicle capable of driving itself from Las Vegas to Los Angeles. Not by road, that would never be allowed, but via the safer route offered by the deserts and scrubland that knitted a patchwork between the two cities. Not that Brooke's test route felt all that *safe* now as she hurtled towards a 400-metre-deep ravine. She checked the moving map to see how much time she had left. The canyon wasn't marked, but she guessed it was the blank section, the all-swallowing featureless bit at the top of the screen, which she'd be reaching in less than thirty seconds.

There is a time for theory and a time for getting your hands dirty, and this mess qualified for the latter. Unstrapping herself, Brooke closed the laptop and wedged it into the door pocket before pulling herself into the driver's seat. In front of her was a steering wheel with a heavy-duty hydraulic arm clamped to it. The arm snaked its way back behind the dashboard where, via a series of cables and pulleys, it terminated at a junction box controlled by one of the computers on the back seat. *But which one?* There were four to choose from, each with backup batteries designed to kick in if they lost primary power. She could pull a cable, but which one? There were thousands of them, making the back-seat wells look like two big vats of multi-coloured spaghetti. The computers were the domain of her dad, MIT's famous robotics professor, J.P. English. But her nutty father hadn't been around recently to keep a check on Brooke's latest, lethal creation. Indeed, the reason why things were looking so decidedly dodgy for Brooke was due, in part, to the fact that Professor English had spent the last few weeks away, attempting to woo funding from a group of Chinese businessmen for his experimental asteroid-mining project.

Grabbing a pair of pliers and a spanner from the leather toolbelt that swung from her hip, Brooke got to work on the heavy-duty control arm, the galvanized steering mechanism that she'd personally designed to manoeuvre the two-tonne vehicle a brutal 400 kilometres.

The first bolt proved stubborn; hopefully the next ten or so would go easier, but a quick heads-up told

Brooke that even her dexterity with a spanner wouldn't save her and the two-million-dollar robo-car.

Through the mud-smeared windscreen she could see the end of the road and a coachload of tourists running for cover.

CHAPTER 4

'Come on, boy! Get a move on!' said Mr Farley, scooping a handful of socks and pants off the floor and throwing them in his son's face on his way past his room.

Jackson had hardly slept, puzzling over the meaning of last night's events. He should have been exhausted but he wasn't. It was certainly strange to have been contacted in that way, but it was also exciting. Very exciting.

He climbed out of bed and was rooting through his drawer for some clean school socks when his dad called from the kitchen.

'You've got a parcel through here. I had to sign for it. If it's another eBay, I want to see that you've sold something first – remember our little chat?'

Jackson definitely didn't remember ordering anything recently. With his mind still buzzing from everything that had happened just a few hours ago, he threw on his ready-made school shirt-and-tie combination and almost wedgied himself as he hurried to put on his trousers which were similarly configured 'To-Go' with boxers already inside. Then he pounded through to the kitchen to see what else lay in store for him.

His dad had laid out breakfast. It was the same arrangement as always: a bowl of Cheerios, a piece of toast with far too much butter on it and a glass of orange juice. It was a morning ritual that hadn't changed in the four years since Jackson's mum had died. It was exactly how she had prepared breakfast, and neither he nor his dad wanted to change it.

'So, what is it?' Jackson's father asked, handing him a box-shaped package.

'I haven't a clue,' replied the twelve-year-old, draining the glass of juice in one big gulp, before scooping up the toast and cereal bowl in one hand and carrying them and the parcel back down the corridor to his room.

He felt bad about not staying in the kitchen and letting his dad see what might be in the parcel, but if it was anything to do with last night Jackson knew he couldn't risk it. His dad's suspicion of the Internet, coupled with his grumpiness at having just arrived home from his night shift, might lead to him making Jackson answer the usual round of questions. *How long were you on the Net last night? Aren't you bored of that blasted game yet? What do you think kids found to do with their evenings before the invention of instant messaging?* There was no time for that this morning.

Using the penknife from his bedside drawer, Jackson scored open the packing tape and peered inside. Through the thick soup of polystyrene chippings, he could see the edge of a small envelope.

'You are a winner!' read the letter, in big blue writing.

You are this month's Blue Storm Games prize winner! Having stacked up the highest number of online hours this month we are proud to present you with a collection of free and exclusive merchandise. Your prize bundle includes: a pen, a limited-edition mobile phone cover and a chance to win some serious cash!

Who on earth is Blue Storm Games? thought Jackson as he dug into the sea of plastic packing material.

The first thing to surface was a pearlescent-blue pen with BLUE STORM embossed along its shaft. Instead of the usual clip, three curious metal rivets lined up along the length of the pen's top, one blue, one red and one chrome. Jackson unscrewed the lid and was disappointed to find a gold-coloured fountain-pen nib. He disliked fountain pens. Despite repeated demands to use them from certain teachers who believed they encouraged a degree of legibility in even the messiest of scribblers, he insisted on using the Fisher Space Pen his mum had given to him. 'My pen writes at minus twenty degrees centigrade. It writes underwater and in the gravity-free vacuum of space … can you do that with a fountain pen?' It was the closest Jackson came to insolence and that's probably why they let it go.

Eager to understand more about the mysterious package, Jackson turned the box upside down. White polystyrene pieces drifted out across the duvet like a mini-avalanche. A little more foraging and he recovered a Manila envelope and a tight roll of bubble wrap bound with tape.

On the outside of the envelope he read, 'Up to £1,000 could be yours in our cash bonanza! Open up and good luck.' He tore open the envelope, revealing a postcard inside with the words 'Ooops! Better luck next time' printed in big black letters on one side. Turning the card over, he found a line of three one-pound coins held in place by tape. He starred quizzically at the golden coins, the jaded smirks of three Queen Elizabeths leering back at him in perfect symmetry. Jackson was disappointed; it didn't look like the package was going to fulfil his expectations after all. But still, there was something strange about it. For a start, he'd never heard of Blue Storm Games. And he found the coins odd too; in the age of Internet shopping and e-commerce, why give coins away to a competition winner – why not a coupon or a voucher? And just three of them? They were hardly worth their weight in postage.

'It's eight fifteen! Get a move on!' boomed his dad from the kitchen, the three hard kicks on the wall deliberately hard enough to make it all the way through the bathroom to resonate in Jackson's wardrobe.

Jackson felt harassed. 'I'm just leaving!' he shouted back, without any intention of complying with his dad's demands until he'd seen everything the package had to offer.

He put the coins aside and, three mouthfuls of bubble wrap later, was cradling the final prize, the phone cover. But the carefully engineered aluminium case in his hands didn't seem at all like a phone cover. It had the weight and feel of a fully functional handset. Jackson flipped open the matt metal clamshell lid. He was sure he was right. The lower section featured a wafer-thin metal keyboard and a raised directional pad that felt solid to the touch. The top section was taken up by a large screen with a tiny camera lens above it and BLUE STORM GAMES etched beside it. He couldn't immediately see how to power it up, but Jackson was certain this was much more than just the phone cover that the competition blurb had promised.

'What have you got there?'

He hadn't noticed his dad in the doorway. 'I . . . I won a competition,' Jackson stammered, his attention still on the phone.

'Come off it! D'you think I was born yesterday. You

know what we agreed about online auctions,' his dad said, adopting the serious tone that Jackson always suspected he was uncomfortable with. Some adults did 'serious' really well, but his dad was rubbish at it. Instead of serious, he was more deadbeat. He did the screwy thing with his eyebrows like some of Jackson's teachers, but while the best of them could easily hit scary with a mere forehead flex, his dad just ended up looking kind of worn out, old, browbeaten.

Jackson smiled and handed him the letter. 'Read this if you don't believe me.'

'I don't know whether I'm supposed to be impressed or not.' Mr Farley sighed. 'My son, rewarded, for wasting his time on the Internet.'

'Remember what Mum used to say,' Jackson said, grinning. 'Time spent doing something you love is never wasted.'

His dad, as usual, had the last word on the matter. 'Yes, well, unless you want to waste some of your precious time in detention, then you'd better get off to school – sharpish! I'm popping out for some milk. You'd better be gone when I come back.'

As soon as the front door shut behind his dad, Jackson placed the pen and the three coins in front of him and flipped the phone back open. He held it up and examined its sleek metal surface more closely. There were the familiar green SEND and red END keys, as well as the number keys in the usual configuration. Above the screen sat the tiny camera lens. But there was a surprising lack of anything else. No apparent way of turning it on, no battery cover, no power socket and no slot for memory or SIM card. As for the back of the phone, it looked like a solid piece of aluminium, its brushed surface only interrupted by a tiny logo embossed in the centre. This wasn't the Blue Storm branding. Jackson looked more closely. The logo was a combination of a capital 'M' and an 'X'. The logo for MeX.

Deep in thought, the sudden ringtone took Jackson so much by surprise that he almost fell off his bed. It was a cheap, tinny ringtone, quite out of character for such a sophisticated-looking handset. And unless Jackson was mistaken, the tune he could hear it playing was 'Rule Britannia'. He composed himself, pressed the answer button and held it to his ear.

'Hello. Who is this?' said a woman's raspy voice on the other end.

'Er . . . you should know, you called me,' replied Jackson, confused.

There was a momentary pause before the woman's voice continued. 'Voice identification positive for Jackson Farley. Initiating data connection . . . Welcome to the MeX network.'

CHAPTER 5

'Brooke,' her mother's voice crackled from the walkie-talkie that was bouncing around on the dashboard. 'Brooke, can you hear me?'

The young engineer was halfway out of the driver's side window, having decided that bailing out was her only option before certain death, and it didn't help that her mother was still prattling through the radio.

'Brooke! The keys . . . take the keys out of the ignition!'

Brooke paused mid-escape, her eyes fixed on the impending precipice of the very big canyon, and realized that actually wasn't a bad idea at all.

Hauling herself back inside, Brooke reached for the ignition and turned the keys. The engine cut out instantly and the steering arm hissed and went limp. She yanked the heavy steering wheel to the left, throwing the vehicle into a dramatic and final broadside.

Brooke emerged through a cloud of dust, a vision in white Converse baseball boots folded at the heel, denim hipsters and a baseball cap with the words 'Spanner Head' written on it. A young boy who had been left behind in the tourist stampede stood open-mouthed in the adjacent car park.

'Hey, kid,' said Brooke, patting herself down as she walked towards him, 'mind if I have a swig of that Coke?'

The boy, who was all of eight, remained frozen as Brooke extended an oily hand and grabbed his drinks can. She necked its contents then crushed it in a fist before handing it back to him.

'Thanks,' she said, before turning to scrutinize the SUV which, now the dust had finally cleared, she could see was no more than a few centimetres from the canyon's edge. The radio spluttered into life again and Brooke could hear her mother fretting from inside the cabin.

'Are you receiving me, honey? Over.'

'Yes, ma'am!' Brooke replied. 'But you'd better come out and pick me up. I swear this tin can is trying to kill me.'

'Roger that. Just wait till I see that damned father of yours,' said Brooke's mother. 'I'll give him a piece of my mind . . . leaving you to finish off that overgrown toaster on wheels. Stay where you are; I'm on my way. Over and out.' It was a mystery to Brooke why her mother felt compelled to use military-speak whenever she used a two-way, or even a mobile phone for that matter. 'Oh, yes,' Mrs English's voice crackled back over the radio. 'FedEx dropped something off for you. You want me to bring it?'

Brooke wondered briefly if this was anything to do with yesterday's mysterious instant-message conversation. She had spent last night, like she spent every night, juggling a hundred instant-message conversations to a thrash-metal soundtrack. She'd thought the Irish chick, Elan, was just peddling something and Brooke had only stuck with her persistent line of questioning because Brooke's uncle had filled her head with the romance of 'the auld country', as he called it. But the extraordinary pop-up had left Brooke staring at her screen, dumbfounded. She'd scoured the Net until the early hours, looking for any information on this MeX organization that could prove the whole thing was a hoax. She'd come up with nothing.

So Brooke English, thirteen-year-old 'wrench monkey', as her dad called her, youngest-ever graduate of the prestigious Centre for Robotic Science at the Massachusetts Institute of Technology (MIT), decided that yes, she would check out this FedEx parcel, just in case it had anything to do with her recent MeX selection.

'OK, thanks, Mom.'

'Over and out,' said her mother.

CHAPTER 6

28

Dear [Headmaster/mistress],

Please excuse [full name] *from* [school/lesson] *on* [day/month/year]. [First name] *is not feeling well and I have decided to keep* [him/her] *at home in bed for the* [morning/afternoon/day].

I will keep a check on [first name]'s *condition and send* [him/her] *to school at the earliest opportunity.*

Kind regards,

[Parent's name]

[Father/Mother full name]

Jackson didn't take skiving lightly. Until the start of this year he hadn't bunked off once. But since starting back after Christmas, things with Tyler Hughes had become hazardous. Hughes was like bad weather; he was always unpleasant, but sometimes he'd whirl himself into a fully fledged storm. Jackson had chosen to stay off school once or twice, while the storm blew itself out. This was a different case entirely. Jackson was sure not even the sick buzz that Tyler Hughes obviously got from publicly humiliating him could beat the adrenalin rush of what was happening to him right now. *He* had been selected by MeX, only *he* was good enough – not Tyler or his overgrown cronies – and Jackson wasn't wasting time at school until he found out exactly what else was involved. He had acquired one or two techniques that helped the process of skiving from school run smoothly; the free email account he reserved for 'special circumstances' was one of them. He logged into the webmail application, pasted the bogus excuse note he'd found by entering 'Excuse Letters' on Google into a new mail, then ticked the OUT OF OFFICE AUTO-REPLY option, just in case his headmaster felt inclined to reply.

'Anyfing else?' The waitress stood over Jackson holding his empty cup, a second-hand tea bag drooping over the side of the saucer like a recently deceased slug.

Jackson had lost count of how long he'd been sitting in the cafe. *An hour perhaps?* 'Another tea, please,' he said. The waitress simultaneously rolled her eyes and chewed her gum. It was as if the two actions were mechanically connected, one roll of the eyes triggering ten chews, then back to the beginning. Jackson suspected that her particular brand of customer service wasn't reserved for kids who bought just two cups of tea an hour.

As the waitress sauntered her way behind the counter, Jackson turned back to the message in the centre of his phone screen, with the three pound coins and the pen on the table in front of him.

The MeX logo had given way to a most peculiar image. The message 'Awaiting Connection' pulsed at the top of the screen above an animated diagram of a one-pound coin. The animation was made up of several frames. First there was the luminous green outline of the coin. This was followed by an image of the coin with its outer edge now forming a ring, inside which the circular centre section was able to spin freely thanks to a tiny axle. Before looping back to the beginning, the shimmering wireframe animation showed arrows flowing in and out of the coin's hollow centre section. The suggestion was clear. It was some kind of tiny storage space.

Jackson picked up one of the pound coins and examined it closely. There was nothing about the coin to suggest it was anything more exotic than plain old legal tender. Holding it with both hands, he pushed down hard on the coin's surface. Nothing. He tried again, this time putting his nail into the raised copper and zinc crown of Her Majesty Queen Elizabeth II. The centre of the coin gave way and, as it flipped open, something fell out from inside the hollow mid-section and bounced on the table.

Jackson picked up what looked like a tiny flesh-coloured half-moon. Turning it in his fingers, he examined the mysterious object close up, waiting for the first whiff of recognition. It was no bigger than a pea, a soft, rubbery, minuscule three-sided potato wedge. In a row along one side were three very small shiny metal rivets, just like the ones along the side of the pen top, blue, red and chrome. It was the strangest thing Jackson had ever laid eyes on and he hadn't a clue what he was supposed to do with it.

He picked up another coin and once again pushed his nail into its face. The coin remained closed. He pressed harder until his thumbnail buckled, making him wince. It seemed that coin number two contained no secret stash; it was a quid, plain and simple.

The third coin was more interesting. It opened with the minimum of force and gave up a disc-shaped plastic screw-top case, fractionally smaller than the coin itself. Jackson carefully unscrewed the top. Inside, floating in a clear gel, was a contact lens.

Beware of cafe toilets, mused Jackson. *We can build ourselves skyscrapers and space stations, but, as far as cafe toilets are concerned, we still live in caves.*

Jackson edged into the narrow, fan-assisted space, accessed via a door in the cafe kitchen. The room, if you could call it that, was so snug he could sit on the toilet seat with the tiny lens case on his knee and simultaneously wash his hands at the overblown soap dish that masqueraded as a sink. He stared at the miniature screw-top case and pondered what he was about to do. It was a peculiar situation. Here he was, skipping school, about to put in his eye a contact lens, sent to him by an organization he'd never heard of, but that seemed to know all about him. The thought of sticking anything in his eye made him cringe. But what was the alternative? How else could he find out what all this was about?

Jackson looked for a towel, but all he found was 'Honk if you love Jesus' etched into the mottled plaster where he suspected a towel holder had once been. Shaking his hands dry, he unscrewed the case and dipped an index finger into the cool gel. The contact lens came out on the tip of his finger. He examined its moist, glassy surface. It was speckless apart from a small grouping of three indecipherable marks etched near the edge. They were so small, it almost hurt to focus on them. Leaning closer to the mirror, Jackson drew a deep breath then popped the lens into his right eye.

It stung like mad. Like his eyelid was on back to front. And whatever Jackson was expecting from the contact lens, it didn't deliver. His vision was twenty-twenty, just like it had been before. Aside from the constant need to blink and the feeling that he'd been caught in a blinding sandstorm, the purpose of the lens was a mystery.

All of a sudden, a cloudy outline flashed up in his right eye and then vanished as quickly as it had arrived. Jackson sat frozen to the toilet seat, waiting for something to appear again. After a minute or two he realized the ridiculousness of his situation. He was sitting on a rancid toilet lid, staring intently at a wall of yellowing tiles and a tower of bog rolls skewered on a mop handle.

He stood up to leave the tiny restroom and again something flashed briefly before his eye. He walked back slowly through the kitchen. With every step the fuzzy silhouette sputtered in and out of vision, blurred and formless like the ghostly after-image from staring too long at a bright light.

Jackson returned to his window seat and tried to work out what was happening. He leaned down to retrieve the handset from his school bag and a vivid translucent rectangle sparked into life. With his hand firmly on the phone, Jackson could now see what looked like a ghostly cinema screen floating in front of him. Even though he could easily see through it, to the table opposite with a wilted daffodil in a Coke bottle, to the uninterrupted line of cars and buses that stretched up the high street out the window, Jackson could also make out the clear, bright screen with the computer-animated image of a woman's face on it. And it looked like she was talking to him.

CHAPTER 7

Wherever Jackson looked, the disembodied ghostly face was there, hanging in space. He couldn't hear her, but she was clearly talking. Next to her was another green wireframe animation, similar to the one he'd seen on his handset. This time it showed the outline of an ear with what looked like the strange little potato wedge from the first coin being placed under a flap of skin at the ear's entrance.

Jackson went to pull the first coin from his trouser pocket, but as his hand left the phone, the screen vanished. He immediately placed his hand back on the handset and the picture quivered back to life. Jackson had a hunch. He grabbed the phone and dropped it into his breast pocket, puffing his chest out to ensure the phone was in contact with his body. Sure enough, the virtual display rematerialized. With his hands now free, he pulled the coin from his trouser pocket, unlocked it as before and removed the small fleshy device.

As he felt the cold metal rivets of the tiny device slide

against the flesh of his inner ear, just as it was pictured in the animation, the woman's voice became loud and clear. '. . . Stealth Communicator. The power for both this and the Retinal Projector is delivered via the handset or a power repeater in one of your coins.' So, his hunch had been correct. The contact lens, or 'Retinal Projector' as the woman called it, and the grommet or 'Stealth Communicator' were powered as long as Jackson was in contact with the handset.

Her voice, that it seemed only Jackson could hear, as clear as a thought, continued: 'The handset can be left near any electrical power source where it will wirelessly drip charge itself.' Half of the cafe was instantly filled by a brilliant green line drawing of a sitting room with bright red phone handsets on top of a television, on the floor near a plug socket and on the closed screen of a laptop.

'The handset power unit will charge in less than an hour. It will hold its charge for around forty hours of continuous use. This presentation will begin again in thirty seconds. Speak at any time to activate speech engine.' The animation was replaced with the MeX insignia.

Jackson turned to look at the counter, the shimmering letter logo acting like a sniper scope. Princess Chewing Gum was dead centre, leaning forward with both elbows on the counter and chatting to a young guy who must have arrived a couple of minutes ago. Jackson determined from his prescription cruddy workboots and plaster-encrusted England football shirt that he must be a builder. Jackson caught the waitress's attention and motioned to his teacup to suggest he'd like another. The waitress rolled her eyes and went back to chatting to her builder boyfriend. *Brilliant!* thought Jackson. *How long will my tea take now?* And in a process that took him just a couple of seconds, Jackson's mathematical blender of a brain took in all the variables that would affect the delivery of his second cup of tea.

Imagining that:

- A was the amount of time the last cup of tea took to arrive in seconds
- J was how long Jackson thought he spent talking
- B was the amount of time builders generally spent chatting when they should be working
- W was the amount of time the waitress spent chatting
- C was how busy the cafe was (measured on a scale from 1 to 5 – with 1 being ghost town and 5 being Piccadilly Circus)
- L, the likelihood of a text arriving for the waitress in the next few minutes (1 to 5, with 1 being unlikely and 5 being definitely)
- T was the time it would take for her to key in a text
- P, the likelihood of text message taking precedence

over the making of Jackson's tea (1 to 5, with 1 being 'Never! The customer is always first' and 5 being 'Customer? What's a customer?')

- And *I*, Jackson's importance as a customer (1 to 5, with 1 being dumb kid with small change and 5 being regular millionaire generous tipper)

Jackson pictured the formula $Tea = A + \dfrac{1}{CI}\left(\dfrac{BW}{J} + LPT\right)$

as the solution to his parched thirst and quickly filled in the relevant values. As far as he could tell, his last tea, *A*, took about 5 minutes or 300 seconds to arrive. Even by his own admission he was generally disinclined to chitchat, so *J* = 1 minute's chat per hour, or 1 second per minute. Jackson knew that builders were famous for spending much of their working day shooting the breeze, so *B* = 10 seconds. It was Jackson's opinion that this waitress could easily spend at least fifteen minutes of every hour jawboning, so *W* = 15. In terms of population, the cafe wasn't far off a ghost town, so *C* = 2. Princess Chewing Gum's seemingly inexhaustible stream of texts showed no signs of letting up, so *L* = 5 and a text took about thirty seconds to reply to, so *T* = 30. And there was no way she was going to put a geeky truant's tea above a text message, so *P* = 5 and *I* = 1.

Jackson crunched the numbers until he had the answer.

Seven hundred and fifty seconds, or twelve and a half minutes. Exactly.

In the time it took most people to stretch out a finger and turn on a calculator, Jackson had processed all the available data and found an answer. He'd always been able to do these kinds of sums in his head. They were like mini-games he could play anywhere; like *Brain Training* without the need for a console. On the way to school he might search for the highest number of consecutive London buses with a prime number on the front of them – the most he'd ever spotted was five: the 37, the 83, the 127, the 109, followed by his school bus, the number 19. Or he would scan the barcodes on food packets for numerical curiosities while he and his dad put the groceries away. He enjoyed the challenge and he liked the feeling that came with a correct answer. It made him feel he had some control over things; while he could be jumped by Tyler Hughes and his gang on his way home from school, or his mother could, one day, just not come home again, there was at least one thing he could rely on.

Jackson checked the time on the yellowing clock above a sandwich toaster with so much cheese congealed round it that it looked like the Fungoid creature from *Dr Who*. It was 10.40 a.m. Given the time he'd already spent in the toilet, he expected to receive his next steaming cup of stew in precisely eight minutes' time. Jackson definitely couldn't wait that long for the surly waitress to grace him with her service before finding out more about MeX. He decided to reactivate the speech engine. 'Er . . . anybody there?'

The MeX logo vanished and the shimmering screen that now hung in front of Jackson juddered, as if its reset button had been pushed. Then it was as if someone had just changed channels. A window popped up in the middle of the screen. It looked like a digital picture of a brick wall. Jackson looked down; the off-white surface of the table was a better backdrop than the grimy cafe counter. As he concentrated, he saw the image was actually a video feed, because the tufts of grass at its base were swaying in the wind.

Three smaller windows appeared around its edge. The two on the left contained a live video feed of what looked like the same person. They showed the face of an Oriental boy, around nine or ten years old, wearing a bright yellow polo shirt. Bizarrely, one of the video boxes showed the boy looking down, reading or typing something, while the other box showed the same boy leaning on his elbow, fiddling with his ear. A streaming video of the same person, doing two different things at the same time. Jackson filed it in his mental inbox under 'weird'. A third window showed the back of a chair with a tweed jacket slung over it.

'Right, let's get this show on the road!' The voice

belonged to a smart-looking man who had just dropped into the vacant chair on the third screen. He was dressed immaculately, in a bright pink shirt with a black-and-white spotted tie. There was something familiar about him – that voice and the fine blond hair that receded at the sides to form a widow's peak. 'Are communications working OK?'

Jackson wasn't sure if he was supposed to answer, but the two versions of the same Oriental boy both nodded and said something in tandem that sounded like '*Un*', which Jackson presumed meant 'Yes'.

'Ah, the Kojima twins,' said the man. As the boy in the first box looked up, Jackson realized 'he' was, in fact, a girl; the identical figures were twins, and the twins were brother and sister.

'I'm in esteemed company, I must say. Is it true you both own identical Ferraris?' said the smart man.

'*Un*,' replied the barely distinguishable pair without offering a smile.

'Remarkable,' said the man, whose colourful clothes and bleached blond hair seemed at odds with his air of authority. 'But you're not old enough to drive them yet?'

'*Un*,' replied the twins in stereo.

'Not problem,' added the girl. 'We buy own road.'

'You have your own road? Fascinating,' noted the man. 'All that time I wasted at Cambridge when I could have been making my fortune playing video games.'

Then the realization dawned on Jackson. The well-groomed leader of this unconventional video chat was Devlin Lear, billionaire computer geek, whose Lear Corporation all but invented the hardware on which the Internet runs.

Devlin Lear and a brother-and-sister professional gaming team? Jackson was in elevated company. Sure, he could turn a quick buck on *Whisper*, if he had to. A healing spell here; a sword there. There was always someone on eBay willing to part with a few pounds to avoid hours of needless game play. You could make hundreds of pounds in a weekend if you knew the shortcuts. But this was nothing compared to the pro-gamers he'd read about in countries like Japan and South Korea. That was a whole different ball game. These Kojima twins probably had pop-star status and earned millions in sponsorship and prize money. So what could all this be about? Jackson wondered if the twins had been contacted in the same strange way he had. Perhaps Lear was putting together an all-star gaming team and he and these twins had been head-hunted for a multimillion-pound sponsorship deal. Or could they have been assembled to test a new Lear Corporation game? He'd read about professional games testers and was fascinated by the idea of being paid to play the latest games all day.

There was an abrupt crackle and Jackson almost fell

off his chair as his head was suddenly filled with a deafening thrash-metal guitar solo. From the screwed-up faces of his floating chat-room companions, it was clear they were just as shocked by the intrusion. A fourth small video box appeared, containing a dancing teddy bear with a studded black leather collar round its neck. Jackson could just make out a hand rocking the stuffed teddy in perfect time to the blaring music.

'Ms English!' Lear's voice cut straight through the music. 'Turn off that infernal racket.'

The music stopped and the headbanging teddy dropped from view, replaced by a dishevelled girl, about Jackson's age, with long shocking-pink hair.

'Intense, perhaps. But I've never heard Nirvana described as "infernal".' As she spoke, something that Jackson suspected was a piercing winked at him from below her lip.

'Allow me to introduce Brooke English, a brilliant young engineer.' Lear made the dryly spoken introduction for the others' benefit. 'But a little challenged in the music department. English, say hello to the Kojima twins, who are joining us from Tokyo, Japan, and Mr Farley from London. At least it should be Farley . . . it's hard to see from the inside of his rucksack . . . or is that your trouser pocket? No, wait a minute, it's your shirt pocket. Am I right?'

Amazed by the floating display, the dancing teddy

bear and the pink-haired rock chick, Jackson hadn't given a thought to the fact that he'd need to be in front of a camera himself if he was going to join in.

'Put the solid coin in your pocket,' said Lear. 'It'll power everything in the same way the handset does. It's a power repeater, you see. As long as the phone is no more than twenty centimetres away, the coin will suck juice from it – then use your skin or clothes to get power to your earpiece and lens.'

Jackson retrieved the coin that had almost claimed his thumbnail and pushed it into his front trouser pocket. He then flipped open the handset and placed it on the table beside his empty mug, its camera lens pointing up at his face.

'Ah, there you are, my dear boy,' said the man who had once famously suggested the Moon as a possible location for the massive computer servers needed for future Internet storage. Jackson recalled the interviewer had treated the suggestion with scorn, but he thought it was inspired.

'What does the face of someone capable of recalling Pi to three hundred decimal places look like?' continued Lear. 'That's what I asked myself when I read your profile. And there you are, Farley, as plain as the rest of us.'

As Jackson smiled sheepishly at the miniature camera, the waitress placed a steaming mug of tea on his table. The clock read 10.48 a.m.

CHAPTER 8

3.14159265358979323846264333279. Pi. It formed effort-lessly in Jackson's mind. Pi accurate to thirty decimal places. He was seven years old when his mother had taught him the party trick that would spark his fascina-tion with maths. She had written a poem in the young Jackson's birthday card and told him that it hid a secret code. If he guessed the code, he could have his present.

> For I must a verse prescribe
> by artful sense and words describe
> rhyming's cryptic chemistry
> bit by bit wiggling free
> circle by circle soon you see
> sketched out in Grecian schoolery

Two days with his head buried in his mother's books and finally the young Jackson recognized a string of numbers as the ones he'd managed to extract from the birthday verse. By counting the characters in each of the rhyme's words and listing them in order, he had uncovered the world's most famous irrational number, Pi. He loved his shiny new BMX, but the discovery of Pi accurate to thirty decimal places was the best present Jackson had ever had.

As for the next 270 decimal places Lear had referred to, well, that was one reason Jackson didn't get out much.

'How do you know that?' Brooke broke into the conversation with her distinctive American twang. 'How do you know he's a . . . a Pi guy? How do you know any of this stuff about us? How did that handset you sent me recognize my voice . . . you been stalking me or something?'

The American girl was echoing Jackson's own thoughts. As far as he was aware, he'd never shared his fondness for mathematics' most famous infinite number with anyone.

'Farley's maths teacher.' Lear smiled knowingly at Jackson. 'He noticed his doodles on a piece of scrap paper. He was very impressed . . . wrote it down in Mr Farley's school file. And your honeyed tones, Ms English?' Lear looked down and Jackson could see he was typing something. 'Ah yes, your voice was recorded at . . . 17.22 on 16 June last year . . . I believe you were talking to a girlfriend about a band called . . . let me see . . . Satan's Curse. At least, I hope it's a band.'

'Yes, they're a band,' said the indignant American. 'And for a billionaire businessman, you seem to have a lot of spare time to spend eavesdropping. What's all this about anyway?'

Jackson was relieved to hear he wasn't the only one in the dark.

'Listening in is a necessary part of our recruitment process,' said Lear. 'We're only trying to safeguard the secrecy of the MeX organization.'

'What is MeX?' said Jackson, throwing the million-dollar question at him.

'Experimental Mechanicals – MeX,' said Lear. 'It started as a pet project to design hardware for law enforcement. Small, unmanned surveillance vehicles that could be used to scout suspect buildings for criminal activity or slip undetected into a gangster's stronghold.'

'Wow, Robocop!' blurted Brooke.

'In a manner of speaking,' continued Lear. 'We soon realized we'd work better on our own. We've been . . . freelance . . . for the last five years.'

Freelance? It was an interesting choice of phrase and Jackson wasn't sure what Lear meant by it. Before his dad had got his job as a security guard, he had been a *freelance* gardener for a few months. Judging by the amount of time his old man had spent watching TV during that time, freelance was just another word for unemployed.

'You . . . vigilante?' asked one of the twins.

'Certainly not,' replied Lear, breaking into a broad grin. 'We still work closely with various government agencies. We just find it easier to do what we do without . . . all that red tape.'

As he continued to speak, the video stream of the brick wall was replaced with a string of photographs and newspaper headlines: 'Serbian Monster Jailed', 'Drug Cartel Crushed', 'Hostage Freed'. There were photographs of smoking buildings, a group of policemen standing proudly in front of a huge pile of guns and rocket launchers, and several aerial shots of city high-rises and camps in forests and deserts. One newspaper picture that caught Jackson's attention was that of a fat handcuffed man with a torn shirt and a big moustache being loaded into a dark blue van with 'Policía' written on the side. Next to him a headline read 'Gotcha Amigo!'

'Criminals. Gangsters. Warlords. Untouched by the laws that are meant to protect us from them. Indulged by the very governments we elect to stop them. Call it what you will, a commitment to justice, to fair play; a hatred of corrupt governments and the dirty games they play. We move in a world of shadows. We are vigilant and virtuous. Where there is chaos, where order cowers beneath a table and freedom lies beaten in the corner, we wreak our mechanical retribution.'

The headlines vanished and the strange brick wall

returned, the grass at its base still swaying gently in the breeze.

What am I doing here? thought Jackson. *What is this nutter going on about? I can't even stand up to Tyler Hughes. How am I supposed to go up against international drug barons and evil-looking dudes with guns?*

'Now, I'm assuming you're all familiar with the concept of tele-robotics?'

Jackson wasn't, but mumbled 'Yes' anyway.

'Sure, honey,' said Brooke, 'it's all I've been doin' for as long as I can remember. It's how you control stuff from a distance. SUVs, planes, whatever you like. Tele-robotics lets you drive 'em around like great big remote-control toys.'

'Yes, well, we don't deal in toys,' said Lear, 'or those vulgar SUVs you're so fond of for that matter.'

Brooke scowled.

Once again the feed of the brick wall in the centre screen was replaced, this time with a blueprint of what appeared to be a flying saucer.

The disc was described in three drawings, one from above, one from below and one from the side. It was smooth, apart from what looked like circular vents around its edge. The view from underneath, however, showed the outline of a large fan in the centre, its blades radiating outwards like spokes on a wheel.

'Say hello to your training rig, the MeX$_1$.'

Both Kojimas let out a gasp that Jackson recognized as the international language of amazement.

'She's a modular reconnaissance vehicle, which means she can be configured for a number of tasks including intelligence gathering . . . the laying of bugs, motion sensing, video work, that type of thing, and some minor defensive assignments. In the scheme of things, MeX$_1$ is a pussycat, my version of a pizza delivery bike, but she'll tie you in knots if you don't stay ahead of yourselves,' Lear went on. 'We use tele-robotic vehicles like these to tackle situations in the far-flung corners of the globe that governments seem too, shall we say, preoccupied, to bother with.'

Tell me I get to fly that thing and I'm in! thought Jackson, as the sleek outline of an aircraft resembling a classic UFO hovered over the tabletop in front of him.

'Our vehicles are designed to be small and agile enough to slip in and get out without anyone knowing they were there. We do make it into the headlines once in a while. At least we do if you know what to look for – some daring hostage rescue attributed to Special Forces. But it'll have been us at the controls. There's no glory when no one's allowed to know you exist.

'The four of you have been selected because you have what our organization considers to be *appropriate psychological profiles* for the kind of work we do. A number-cruncher, two distinguished cyber athletes and a wayward . . . but brilliant engineer. The question is, do the four of you want to make a difference? How about you, Miss English? I realize you're not short on exotic gizmos, but I can offer you a machine that actually works.'

Brooke opened her mouth, as if she wanted to give Lear a dressing-down for yet another example of his uninvited 'eavesdropping', but then she seemed to think better of it. 'Yada yada. I'm in, as long as they come in other colours. Military grey is so last season.'

Lear chose, perhaps wisely, not to respond.

'And, Farley,' Lear continued, 'don't tell me you wouldn't appreciate a little intrigue and adventure. You trudge back and forth to that school of yours every day, but can you say you feel stretched by the experience? Isn't that, and the unwanted attention your *brainy* status brings you, the reason you play hooky so often?'

Was it a compliment or a criticism? Jackson wasn't sure. It made his cheeks flush all the same. He wasn't a truant. He didn't want the others thinking that. He just took a few days off each term to . . . deal with things. And he wasn't a pushover either; he could look after himself, as long as the person doing the pushing wasn't twice his size, which Tyler Hughes patently was.

It was hard attending a school where it seemed most of the other kids were more interested in listening to music, or filming each other with their mobile phones doing stupid stunts, than listening to what was said in class. Jackson was no swot, at least he didn't think he was, but he liked most lessons and that marked him out as a target. Sometimes it seemed to him that unless you liked exactly the same things as everyone else, spoke the same, watched the same TV shows and showed the same brutality to those lower down the school food chain, you were treated like an outcast.

There were exceptions: Amisha could be a bit weird, but she always had time for a conversation about space and the possibilities of alien life, and Sarah Jacobs had invited him to go into town with her on more than one occasion; he hadn't taken her up on the offer, but it was nice to be asked.

He got on best with the other members of the chess club: Taylor Dillon, who he'd sometimes met up with at The Zap Shack cyber cafe to play *Whisper*, until his dad had suspended Taylor's account after he'd bought thousands of MP3s with his credit card, and Otis Gibbs, who was quite a bit younger than Jackson, and awarded him a degree of hero worship on account of his chess skills. But even the people he considered friends would ignore him when certain ringleaders were handing out the beatings and that's when Jackson would make himself scarce.

Brooke gave Jackson an awkward grimace as he struggled to find a witty reply to deflect Lear's very personal question, just like Brooke had done. But he couldn't think of anything good to say.

In any case, if he was honest with himself, Lear had it about right. After all, why was he here? Why was Jackson sitting in a cafe in the middle of a school day? And he wasn't just curious about MeX now. This gear was more than simply cool. Did he really want to turn down the opportunity of a lifetime?

'Why not?' he said coolly, as if enlisting in a top-secret organization was no big deal.

'And what of our gaming duo? Does the thought of doing something your father doesn't control excite you?'

The Kojima twins eyed Lear sternly, as if they considered what he had said to be the height of rudeness. It *was* rude, thought Jackson, sharing details of their relationship with an overbearing father. But Jackson had to hand it to him: Lear's tactic of using the information he had gathered to push personal buttons had worked on him and Brooke. Master Kojima flicked his head towards his sister and whispered something in her ear. She continued to stare with an intensity that was no doubt intended for Lear.

'What is . . . capability of vehicle you show?' asked the young Japanese girl in her stilted English.

'I'm afraid I can reveal nothing more unless you agree to join us. What I will say is that it will test even your considerable skills as gamers. So, what is your answer?'

Again Master Kojima whispered something into his sister's ear before the two of them turned, bowed in unison and said '*Un.*'

'Very well,' Lear continued smoothly. 'It's time for you to grab your pens.'

CHAPTER 9

Jackson dug the blue fountain pen out of his school bag. As he held it up to examine it, he was reminded of his surroundings. The swooning couple behind the counter were still far too interested in each other to worry about the last of the big spenders playing with his new pen in the window seat.

'Note its bejewelled elegance,' Lear said, holding up an identical pen and running his finger along the three coloured spots on the pen top. 'But also beware, for these are magic stones.' Jackson wondered if Lear used this kind of flowery language all the time, or if he just put it on for new recruits.

Lear pulled the top off, exposing the nib, and pushed it on to the other end of the pen. He then closed his hand round it and held it out in front of himself.

Jackson checked his surroundings once more before self-consciously mimicking Lear's actions.

'It's called a *gestural interface*; a magical combination of nano-engineered components that can turn just about anything into a magic wand!' Lear flourished the pen in mid-air and the blueprint in Jackson's view was instantly replaced by the view of the brick wall, now swaying in time with Lear's gestures.

'They say the pen is mightier than the sword. Well, when it's configured as a joystick and wirelessly jacked into one of my robots . . . it's mightier still.'

Holding the pen steady in the palm of his hand, Lear appeared to nudge it gently backwards towards himself. The brick wall zoomed further away, until Jackson could see it was one side of a derelict building. It was now apparent that the central video feed of the wall was coming from a camera mounted on a MeX_1 robot that Lear was controlling.

Suddenly the view lurched forward as Lear sent the remotely controlled vehicle on a high-speed tour of an abandoned junkyard. Up high and over the brick wall, skimming the top of a rusty corrugated roof, then down towards two rotten garage doors. With a twist of the pen, he flipped the MeX_1 on its side and it darted through the doors to a ramshackle workshop, flying past a heap of old tyres and a precarious wall of oil barrels. Then, Jackson realized, Lear must have flicked the craft's nose up because the screen was now pointing towards the building's roof, the dust kicked up by the vehicle's fan sparkling in the shafts of sunlight that streamed through the spaces left by missing metal tiles.

Lear spoke calmly as the vehicle he was controlling flew upwards and burst through the largest gap in the roof into bright sunshine.

'MeX$_1$ is controlled using a combination of inputs from the floating pen – and vocal mimicry.'

'Vocal mimicry?' asked Jackson.

'Pretending to speak. Mouthing words without actually saying anything,' replied Lear, the roller-coaster view unrelenting as he threw the machine underneath rusted farm machinery and in and out of a line of dilapidated caravans. 'The grommet in your ear measures subtle changes in pressure in your inner ear when you mouth certain keywords,' he continued. 'Try saying the word "Menu", but don't let any sound come out.'

Jackson did as instructed and a list of words appeared down the left of the floating screen: VIEW, MAP ARM, SET-UP, SPEC, EXIT.

'That's buff!' said Brooke, who had obviously just tried the silent voice control for herself.

The Kojima twins were mumbling in hushed Japanese; the wonderment on their faces was obvious.

Jackson mouthed 'View' and a video feed from another craft popped up, looking as if it sat waiting for him inside an old shed. With effortless flexes of his jaw, Jackson found he was cycling through the options menu of his very own MeX$_1$ – ARM: BASS BOMB, CAMERA, DAZZLER.

'Word of warning, ladies and gents,' said Lear, bringing his remote vehicle into a controlled hover, 'don't waste any of your defensive measures just yet –'

He hadn't finished his sentence when there was a blinding flash that caused everyone to reel back.

'Holy moly!' said Brooke. 'What was that?'

'*Virtute non armis,*' said Lear. 'It's our motto. It means "Virtue not by force of arms". What you just witnessed was the Dazzler, one of two non-lethal weapons that your MeX unit carries. We have what is called a non-lethal mandate, an international agreement allowing us to operate as long as our machines don't use lethal force. The Dazzler has a range of about twenty-five metres and is designed to overwhelm the electronics and computer systems of our enemies with a pulse of electromagnetic energy – and it'll temporarily blind any human opponents that get in its way.

'Before Farley got trigger happy,' Lear continued, 'I was trying to explain that the Dazzler and Bass Bomb can only be used once each. So, Farley, you're already one weapon down.'

'Er . . . sorry about that,' said Jackson. He wondered if the others felt as astonished as he did about the dangerous weapons their vehicles were carrying.

'Apologize to English, not me; she's your teammate,' said Lear.

'Teammate?' asked Brooke.

'It's you two versus the Kojimas.'

Jackson saw the twins look at each other, whisper something he couldn't interpret, and then perform some kind of complicated handshake before gently banging their foreheads together. They seemed nice enough, but judging by what he assumed was the gaming duo's little warrior jig, they would be serious competition.

'What're we playing?' asked Jackson.

'To use the video-gaming parlance you're so fond of,' answered Lear, 'I believe it's called a deathmatch.'

CHAPTER 10

'I think the idea is for you to take pieces out of them, not me,' said Brooke.

Jackson's MeX bot was zigzagging its way down a narrow alley made up entirely of old engines, bouncing like a lunatic pinball off every available surface, including Brooke's machine.

Lear's idea was that a deathmatch offered the ideal opportunity for the four recruits to get to grips with the MeX$_1$. 'You can fly them around an assault course for as long as you like,' he said. 'But until someone's trying to blow you out of the air, you'll never really learn what these machines can do.'

So far Jackson had found the whole experience electrifying, despite the fact that he couldn't seem to fly his robotic saucer in a straight line. His partner, on the other hand, was having no trouble at all keeping her craft straight and he was determined not to let her down.

'You need to be more gentle with the controls, cowboy,' continued Brooke.

Holed up in her workshop at the English family ranch in a remote corner of California, the young American was speaking from the salvaged three-seater of an old 1960s Cadillac on which she was lying with Green Day's *American Idiot* plugged into one ear, and the MeX grommet in the other. The ancient car bench was usually reserved for watching movies after one of Brooke's mammoth workshop sessions. She had been known to work twenty-four hours flat if she couldn't solve a problem. Tonight, however, it wasn't a movie that had her hooked, but the virtual adventure in which she was a main protagonist.

'I'll get the hang of it, thanks very much,' replied Jackson. The pen was amazing; it was as if it was tethered by wires to the machine he was controlling. Even the slightest flex of his finger muscles would register as a dip or the beginnings of a roll. Jackson found he could improve his control of the flying machine by resting his elbow on the cafe table. And he needed the improvement. Neither Jackson nor Brooke had seen or heard from the Kojimas since Devlin Lear bade battle commence. Already a Dazzler down, Jackson could only hope that the brother and sister duo weren't camping round the next corner.

Jackson expanded his 'cockpit' window to fill his view and Lear's smooth tones filled his ear like a TV voice-over.

'The medium that carries your gestures from the pen to the robotic machines you are controlling is the Internet. During their development we referred to them as *remobots*. But I've always preferred the more staccato 'dot.robot'. Call it a fringe benefit of owning your own network of satellites, but I can drop a MeX unit anywhere on the planet inside twenty minutes.'

'Wait! You drop these things in from space?' said Jackson.

'Absolutely.'

Jackson recalled the Lear Net advert that had launched their world-famous Satellite Internet Service. Lear's *Surf the Skies* campaign was heralded as a great success for bringing the wonders of the Web to some of the poorest and most remote parts of the globe.

'Your dot.robots are electrically powered,' Lear informed them exuberantly. 'They get the juice for their ducted fan engines from fuel-cell batteries. Flaps on their underside allow them to hover and move locations by vectoring the flow of air. Oh, and try not to crash. They are a single-use solution, throwaway you might say.'

'A throwaway robot?' asked Brooke. 'Not exactly environmentally friendly.'

'In point of fact it's one hundred per cent disposable. Just a puff of smoke . . . and a super-heated fireball . . . and hey presto, it's like it never existed!'

Hearing how sophisticated his machine was made Jackson feel all the more stupid for being such a dodgy pilot. He managed his first controlled turn into a narrow corridor made entirely of railway carriages stacked four high on either side. Luckily, the Kojimas were nowhere to be seen as his machine continued to swagger like a drunk.

'Try the MAP option in your menu,' suggested Lear.

Jackson mouthed the required command and a circular grid materialized at the bottom of his display.

'The outer ring covers a distance of fifty kilometres, the inner ring just a hundred metres. It uses a combination of infrared and radar signals to pick out you and your adversaries.'

'Cool,' exclaimed Brooke. 'So, Farley, have you tamed that tiger yet or am I gonna have to do this on my own?'

'Don't worry about me,' said Jackson. 'It's that spot in the middle of your map you need to be concerned with.'

Two icons blinked in the inner circle of Jackson's glowing grid display, like a couple of flies stuck in a brilliant spider's web. The one at the very centre was obviously Brooke's machine and was clearly labelled 'English', but the other symbol near it denoted one of the twins' machines, 'Kojima', followed by an unrecognizable squiggle that floated mystifyingly beside it.

'That's odd,' said Jackson. 'I'm only seeing one of the twins.'

'Me too. D'you think the other one is running scared?'

'Knowing the twins' zeal for virtual combat, I'd say that's unlikely,' Lear interrupted. 'I'll wager one of them has discovered stealth mode.'

Stealth mode, thought Jackson. *How did I miss that?*

'It's not too effective if you're moving . . . but when your bot is stationary, it'll render it almost invisible to radar.'

Jackson found the STEALTH command buried in his menu. While the silent instruction was still skipping across his lips, the centre circle of Jackson's web display dimmed and a moment later Brooke's icon vanished. Now they were both in stealth mode, hidden from the Kojimas' displays. Strange, then, that one of the twins had decided to remain conspicuous.

'I've got an idea,' said Jackson. 'Brooke, d'you see that square on your one o'clock?'

The precisely drawn glowing square on the grid was actually an area of muddy wasteground boxed in by the carcasses of three articulated lorries. The large containers on the back of each battered truck looked ready to spew their contents into the square, a curious mixture of entangled exhaust pipes hanging out of the side of the first lorry, neat piles of copper wire in the second and what looked like hundreds of sofas jammed inside the third.

Years spent playing first-person-shooter games online had taught Jackson a few tricks. For example, a simple tactical advantage could be gained by leaving behind a teammate in an enclosed space with only one entrance. The rest of the team would then work to herd their unsuspecting opponents through the entrance where their crack-shot comrade would pick them off. It was also the surest way to get a player booted off a server and labelled a 'camper', but this was life and death, sort of, and gaming etiquette would have to take a back seat. Jackson just wasn't sure how Brooke would respond to being the one left behind.

'I get it. Leave the broad behind so you can go get all the glory? No way, José! You stay behind if you want to. I'm gonna go lasso me a robot.'

Brooke wasted no time, accelerating away from Jackson in the direction of the twin's signal, her remobot skimming the bonnets of the rust buckets that lined her route.

Jackson jabbed the pen in his hand forward, the view in front of his remobot twisting violently as he flicked the craft up and over Brooke's machine, the two craft ending up nose to nose.

'Whoa, rein in your horse there, skip,' said a startled Brooke, the lift fan underneath her MeX_1 throwing up a cloud of dirt and stones as she braked hard to avoid collision.

'Brooke, I want to win this as much as you do and we can, but only if we work as a team,' urged Jackson. 'Trust me, I just need you to hang back.'

Brooke hesitated for a tense moment, her robot saucer drifting slowly in front of Jackson's, its grey profile like the shadow of a huge manta ray stalking the cafe table where he'd now been seated for some three hours. Jackson glanced in the waitress's direction to make sure he wasn't being stared at. Her boyfriend had gone and she now had a queue of two customers to deal with, but that didn't stop her talking into her mobile while she poured their drinks and buttered their toast.

'All righty,' Brooke broke the silence. 'As my dad says, the best thing about following orders is that you get to blame someone else when everything goes wrong.'

Not exactly a vote of confidence, but green light enough for Jackson to pitch his MeX$_1$ forward and race towards the blip with the twins' name and that curious symbol. What was it? A '4'? An 'R' perhaps . . . a capital 'R'? He hoped his hunch was right, but for now Jackson had more immediate things to worry about. Narrowly avoiding random pieces of jagged steel and open doors that blocked the endless car-lined corridors, he sped towards the location of the symbol. Jackson slowed down a few metres from it and decided he had been right – it was an upper-case 'R'. 'Kojima R'. He was sure of it.

It was time to let Brooke know. 'What do you get if you put 1 and 2 together?'

'Er . . . 3?' said Brooke.

'No, I mean if you put one over the other?'

Brooke, who like her teammate had been puzzled by the mystery of the disappearing twin and that strange squiggle, gasped. 'An "R"! Kojima 1 and Kojima 2 on top of one another looks like Kojima "R". Jackson, this is a trap!'

●CHAPTER 11

Jackson had known all along. He observed the shadowy outlines of his opponents hovering in a nearby doorway, the first saucer a metre or so above the ground, the second piggybacking just millimetres above it: one radar symbol, two robots.

He had the twins just where he wanted them. It might be two against one, and Jackson might only have one Bass Bomb left, but he had the element of surprise.

'Brooke, it's time we played them at their own game. Switch your stealth mode on and off a few times – you need to make them think your system is malfunctioning,' he ordered.

'Very devious, Mr Farley,' said Lear, suddenly back in Jackson's ear and evidently observing their every move. 'I wasn't sure you had it in you.'

Jackson decided to wait and see what happened before taking any credit.

'How's that, captain?' asked Brooke, her icon flashing sporadically on and off Jackson's map.

Jackson was watching the twins who, after being practically motionless for the last few minutes, had suddenly moved in the direction of Brooke, holding their stacked formation flawlessly.

'Perfect! They're heading straight for you, Brooke!' Jackson shadowed the pair from a distance as they followed a river of wire and cables that carved a route around towers of old TVs and computer monitors.

'Just bring Donner and Blitzen to me. I'll give them a hillbilly welcome they'll never forget!'

Brooke was ready for action. She had managed to slide her craft inside the canvas sheeting that covered the back of one of the trucks. Using her remobot's nose to shunt a couple of exhausts out of the way, her machine was hidden but still offered a clear view of the entrance to the square. Below that the spider's web display showed what still appeared as just the one Kojima, steadily approaching.

'Stand by, Brooke . . . two Kojimas, incoming. Give 'em everything you've got!'

It was all Jackson could do to keep pace with the devious double act, who despite maintaining their tricky flight pattern, were pushing their machines to the limit. Jackson's bot bucked fiercely as he banked round the final bend, glancing off a windowless double-decker bus while he levelled out for the final straight.

'Better drop anchor, skipper,' advised Brooke, 'it's about to get bomb-diggity in here.'

Jackson eased back on the small controller in his hand just in time to see the twins break formation, one darting left underneath a jumble of fridges and the other coming to a stop at the entrance.

'Brooke . . . they've split up!' warned Jackson. But the phrase was lost in an ear-splitting boom that had him leaping out of his chair. His yell caused a group of workmen who had just walked into the cafe to abruptly stop talking and burst out laughing.

Jackson turned his back on them, cradling his throbbing ear in his hand. It felt like the grommet had detonated on his eardrum, the thunderous aftermath of the bang bouncing around inside his skull. Even his virtual display was affected, the view out of the front of his machine shuddering and shifting for a good few seconds.

'Yehaa!' As Brooke let out the triumphant cry, a crippled MeX$_1$ robot came tumbling backwards towards Jackson, sparks flying from its underside as it ricocheted uncontrollably between the walls of the narrow, improvised passageway.

'Ah, the Bass Bomb,' said Lear. 'Its very battle-cry is forged of sonic fury.'

'That thing is off the hook!'

'Indeed it was, Ms English. It produces a low-frequency shock wave capable of blowing an opponent back. And for your future reference, it will seriously impair a human target, usually making them defecate.'

'Eugh!' said Brooke

Jackson brought his vehicle alongside the stricken saucer. He knew that with one command he could end Master Kojima's attempts to recover and put himself and Brooke in the lead. But the bot looked so helpless, twitching and jerking like a fish marooned on a mudbank.

'We must not allow ourselves to be drowned by fear, Farley, but hold our chins aloft and fight!'

Jackson felt a wave of frustration. He wasn't scared. But hitting the twin when he was down didn't seem right. Nevertheless, this was a 'deathmatch' and if that's what was required, then so be it.

No sooner had Jackson's lips begun to form the fire command than there was a sudden burst of light, vivid flashes of azure and turquoise that threatened to set alight Jackson's right eye. As the effects of the Dazzler wore off, Jackson saw the fuzzy outline of a revitalized Kojima bot escaping through the gap its teammate had found earlier.

'Why didn't you toast that sucker when you had the chance?' asked Brooke, who had been struggling to free her craft from a farrago of tail pipes and had just made it out of the square, only to see the craft she thought she'd scuppered slip away.

'I thought he was out for the count . . . it . . . it didn't seem fair.' Jackson was suddenly realizing that he was the only one who was thinking this way. He was going to have to toughen up.

'It's the shielding . . .' Lear's voice interrupted Jackson's thoughts.

'The what?' Jackson asked.

'The vibration from Brooke's Bass Bomb blast would wreck most conventional electronic devices, but your robots are shielded. So, if you want to KO the Kojimas, Farley, you'll need to get closer next time.'

'I'll get so close, they'll be able to smell what I had for breakfast.' And with that, Brooke was off, her MeX₁ shooting past Jackson's and plunging under the space in the fridge pile. Jackson followed suit, tipping his machine into a dive and giving chase.

'They must be in there,' declared Brooke. With no trace of the twins on their maps, she and Jackson had spent the last ten minutes scouring every centimetre of the scrapyard. They were hovering outside a crumbling barn, the entrance to which was shrouded in strips of jagged plastic that looked like yellowed teeth in the giant mouth of a demon. 'Whatcha wanna do now, master chief?'

'Get in there and finish this thing!'

'Booya!' yelled Brooke.

Jackson was done with planning; he'd taken an eye-load of Dazzler, his ear was still aching and, worst of all, he'd been outmanoeuvred at every stage.

The two saucers slipped silently through the plastic teeth and into the gloomy building. The barn was bare but for the outline of a monster combine harvester in the beams of light from gaps in the wooden cladding. Jackson's machine cruised slowly past a few scattered hay bales, none of which looked a fit hiding place.

'Would you look at that . . . a 1969 Ford Mustang.'

Jackson sent his bot over to Brooke's, which was hovering a few metres away from a collection of old tyres and hubcaps.

'You can tell which cars those rusty old things belonged to?' said Jackson, looking at the line of metal discs propped against an old workbench.

'Yes, siree. I read 'em like headstones. The big red ones are from a Chevy and the ones in the middle are from a European Ford . . . I'm guessing early 1970s.'

'What about these?' Jackson was pointing the nose of his vehicle at two grey discs at the end of the line of hubcaps. No sooner had he asked the question than he realized what he was looking at.

The Kojima saucers sprang from the darkness and, before Jackson had time to think, the harsh glare of a Dazzler seared his eyeball. It was all the more unbearable because he couldn't cry out as the cafe in which he sat had filled up with lunchtimers. So he just writhed in his plastic chair and watched helplessly as his MeX$_1$ was engulfed in a flare of electrical energy, sparks fanning out like a Catherine wheel as it spun wildly before flipping on to the workbench.

'Bravo, Master Kojima!' declared an obviously impressed Lear. 'But the deathmatch doesn't end until all weapons have been expended or your dot.robots are incapacitated!'

'I'm afraid I'm licked!' Brooke's vehicle had been flung violently backwards during the melee, toppling over a stack of wooden pallets, several of which now had the bot pinned down. Not that she could have done much anyway; her savaged electronics were now incapable of delivering anything more than a few defiant twitches.

Jackson was moving his pen around every axis in attempts to find enough lift to right his capsized craft. His efforts were fruitless and all he could do was look on, upside down, as the two Kojima robots floated towards Brooke to finish her off.

'Now would be a good time to serve up that Dazzler you've been saving, Brooke.'

'I'd love to, skip, but my electrics are fried!' Jackson realized that Brooke's saucer had absorbed most of the Dazzler's magnetic pulse. There was only one thing he could do.

Jackson's Bass Bomb surprised everyone, not least Brooke.

'What the heck are you doing!' she bellowed over the din.

But Jackson's plan was working. Billows of sonic vibration broke across the surface of his machine, causing it to jiggle along the bench's wooden surface like a jumping bean and eventually fall off. The moment it tipped over the edge and the powerful lift fan finally had some air to chew on, the robot saucer launched itself across the barn, glancing the side of the combine before hitting the twins and scattering them like skittles.

Jackson completed a whirlwind circuit of the barn before pulling his Mex$_1$ into a breakneck vertical climb which saw the twins form up on his tail. With the Japanese hot shots now mirroring his every move, he knew it was only a matter of time before they unleashed their final salvo.

'A game of cat and mouse, Mr Farley.' Lear sounded intrigued. 'The only question is, which one are you?'

'Neither, as it happens!' said Jackson. 'You ready, Brooke?'

'I guess so, cap'n.'

Jackson reached the apex of his climb and, with the nose of his MeX$_1$ kissing the rafters, let the robotic aircraft stall and fall on to its back, gravity and the full-throttle-ducted turbofan driving it downwards.

'OK, bring up your menu. There's something special in there.' Jackson wasn't sure if the Kojimas could hear, so he was keeping things cryptic.

'Say what?' Brooke pondered for a couple of seconds. 'Oh sure, I see what you're about, you sly ol' dawg.' She had opened the SPEC tab in her menu, guessing it was an abbreviation for 'Special' and was now staring at Jackson's plan.

As his remobot pulled out of the dive, Jackson's forward view trembled while the craft's advanced thermoplastic airframe struggled to cope with the extreme velocity. Straight and level now, his MeX_1 screamed towards the pile of wooden pallets before streaking straight over the top of Brooke's stranded machine. Jackson looped upwards to see the Kojimas pulling out of their dive. As the twins passed just millimetres above Brooke's saucer, there was an almighty explosion. All three machines and most of the pallets were lost in a furious fireball.

When the smoke cleared, a blackened halo on the barn floor marked the spot where the three remobots had met their fiery fate. Fragments of wood and part of the workbench were still smouldering, but there was no visible trace of anything robotic.

'Hot-diggity-damn!' yelped Brooke. 'Now that's what I call barnstormin'!'

'Of course, the idea of keeping the incendiary device

under SPECIALS and not ARM is to avoid an accidental discharge. But I'm guessing that was no accident?' It was clear Devlin Lear was impressed with the pair's unconventional use of the MeX$_1$'s self-destruct feature.

Jackson felt a flush of pride.

'You betcha, daddio,' said a jubilant Brooke. 'Well, if you're having a barbecue – it's rude not to share.'

'I commend you both on a prudent win. But I'm not sure what your Japanese fellow-fighters will have to say about it.'

'*Isseki ni chou.*' It was the voice of Master Kojima. At least Jackson thought it was, as the duo not only looked the same, they sounded very similar.

'It mean . . . one stone, two birds. It is old Japanese saying. My brother paying compliment. We look forward to flying with you – not at you.'

Jackson was about to repay the compliment when a third voice cut in.

'I'm sick of little cretins like you taking the Michael. Order a full English breakfast or sling yer hook.' It wasn't a Japanese saying and it definitely wasn't a compliment. The cafe girl's face loomed large in Jackson's virtual display.

CHAPTER 12

Theoretically, Jackson's iPod could hold a maximum of five thousand songs. In reality, it held six hundred and twenty-three songs, forty-one podcasts and thirteen *Dr Who* audio books rented and then ripped from the town library. What's more, Jackson could recall the precise numerical position of each of them. He had no choice as, thanks to Tyler Hughes, the screen of his pulverized player no longer worked – it was completely blank. If, for example, he wanted to find a particular song, it was a matter of moving his finger around the player's click-wheel in a precise sequence. The first 'click!' sound always meant he was in the MUSIC menu; a further three clicks of the dial would bring him to the SONGS folder. It was then a case of remembering the position of a tune – say, the two hundred and twenty-third song – U2's 'Vertigo'. So the number code Jackson needed to remember for his favourite U2 track was 13223.

He could find anything on his machine by recalling its combination, then counting out the clicks as he turned the wheel like a rotary lock on a safe. Madonna's 'Like a Virgin', his mum's favourite, was 13564. Dr Who's 'Agents of Algore' equalled 1512 and the folder containing his much-favoured NASA podcasts was 17, and then whatever number podcast he was after from 1 to 41.

Of course, he was missing out on album art or the chance to watch music videos and TV shows on his device like some of the other kids, but Jackson's music number system had some added benefits. It meant that for most of the last term he had been able to covertly access his music library during class without the need to pull his iPod out of his pocket. He'd even stripped a headphone so it was barely noticeable when secreted in one ear.

Today, however, it wasn't a hotwired headphone kept in place with a bit of tape and skin-coloured modelling clay that was stuck in Jackson's ear, but the undetectable and considerably more comfortable MeX grommet.

After the training match Lear had spoken briefly about their first mission. He said he would review the footage from their machines afterwards and debrief them, but that from now on he would not be there during missions to assist them. From now on the team members were on their own.

To help them prepare Lear had given the four conscripts access to the Experimental Mechanicals network. All they were required to do was call a mobile phone number, wait for a dead tone and hang up. They'd then receive a call back and a vocal-identity check. This gave them entry to MeXnet with its blisteringly quick Internet access and to MeX's own internal network on which Lear had left them some files, which he referred to as 'a little homework'.

They had not been told when their services would be needed, but simply instructed to keep their MeX gear with them at all times and wait to be contacted. It was all rather mysterious. In fact, just what Jackson had signed up for – *intrigue and adventure*, as Lear had put it.

There was nothing 'little' about Lear's homework. The MeX manual was a three-hundred-page guide that detailed everything the MeX operator needed to know about the dot.robots and their sophisticated support network.

In addition there was a large collection of mission documents and photographs, which described a group of guerrilla fighters called The Faces. The group were responsible for a series of bombings in and around the Siem Reap province of Cambodia. They were said to live a nomadic existence, setting up temporary camps, living among the jungle ruins of the county's ancient Khmer civilization, performing hit-and-run bombing raids that, so far, the authorities had been unable to prevent. They got their name from the tattoos that adorned their faces: cryptic Khmer symbols and images of animals cut into their skin with knives and ink.

These fierce-looking fighters were at the heart of the new recruits' first mission for MeX. Excitement – and fear – had kept Jackson awake most nights since they'd first been briefed about it. Even now he struggled to divide his attention between the mission material he could see floating in front of him and Mr Willard, his history teacher.

The teacher was busy writing three sentences on the whiteboard: *Is it a bird? Is it a plane? No, it's a cow!*

But Willard was actually Jackson's favourite teacher and for that reason he tried to focus on the lesson the teacher was about to deliver. The connection with Willard had been kick-started after discovering a shared passion for codes and code-breaking. It had been in a lesson on Second World War cryptography. 'The cracking of codes won us the war,' Willard had said. Jackson loved the idea that V2 rockets and Spitfires were bit players while the real secret weapons of the Second World War were the code-cracking mathematicians. Willard, who gave all his lessons a headline or catchphrase, had started that one by writing 'Even geeks can be superheroes' on the whiteboard. Jackson had liked that idea even more. After class, Jackson had told his teacher about a musty linen-bound book in a box of his mum's things. The book had belonged to her father, his granddad, and was called *The*

Bletchley Bombe. The antiquarian hardback told the story of a fantastic calculating machine designed by English mathematician Alan Turing to smash the heavily encrypted radio transmissions of the Nazis.

Willard had used their mutual admiration of Alan Turing to try and persuade Jackson to join his chess team.

'Alan Mathison Turing was a mathematical superhero. He's also the father of modern computer science – but I'm getting sidetracked – the point is that he wrote what many believe was the first ever computer chess program. Except of course there wasn't a computer powerful enough to run it . . .' For a moment Willard looked to have confused himself. 'What I'm trying to say, Farley, is that Turing was a genius mathematician just like you. But he was ghastly at chess! If you could learn to win at chess – the game of kings, Farley – you'd be better than Turing.'

It wasn't the argument that Jackson found persuasive, but the passion of the teacher who always wore the same bad clothes and never failed to make him laugh. In truth, Jackson's first year in the school chess team was marked by a litany of embarrassing failures, one to a six-year-old girl which Jackson unsuccessfully campaigned to have annulled on grounds that she wasn't even of school age. But Jackson had risen to the challenge, absorbing the thousands of 'plays' of the grandmasters that had been transcribed online by loyal chess fans. Within a year of picking up his first pawn, it was one of Jackson's games that won his school the County Cup.

Willard turned round from the board at the front of the classroom and held up a textbook with a picture of a very sick-looking cow.

'This bovine has the plague,' he said. 'What possible use could a sick cow have in a siege situation?'

Jackson saw that no one had their hand up.

'Violet. You're good at French. What's this?'

Willard sketched a childlike drawing of a device that looked like some kind of medieval see-saw: a triangle with a couple of wheels on the bottom and a big stick balancing on top, hastily sketched speed-lines suggesting motion.

'It's a trebuchet, Sir,' said Violet Poole confidently.

Willard now added a rather sorry-looking stick-figure cow being hurled from the medieval machine, even taking the time to add a daisy to its mouth which met with a ripple of laughter. He then wrote 'Biological Warfare' in red marker.

Jackson focused back on the MeX mission documents. The phantom pages could be shunted around the room by minuscule movements of Jackson's eyeball.

He pulled up a photograph of one of the jungle fighters, the pages revolving like the numbers on a ghostly roulette wheel, until a translucent tattooed face hung in front of Willard's whiteboard. The image of the man's face made him jump. He had a set of extra eyes drawn on his forehead. Jackson thought they looked incredibly realistic as they stared back at him. There was no less detail in the fists that were etched into each cheek and the flames that threatened to consume his nose.

Jackson didn't like the way the photo made him feel. There was something disturbing in the act of marking your own face, something that made the man inhuman. He remembered how he'd felt when Lear had shown the four of them the newspaper headlines and given them the 'justice and fair play' speech. Jackson had been hooked by the notion that he might get to do some good. Perhaps even more, that what he would do, would make people sit up and take notice. That was something Jackson hadn't really ever experienced before. But the sinister man's face reminded him that this was a serious business. He looked across the classroom and found Tyler Hughes. Compared to the man in the photograph, he didn't look that scary at all.

Jackson brought a document into view with the words 'Intelligence Report – MeX Eyes Only' stamped above it.

According to the report, The Faces were planning to plant IEDs or Improvised Explosive Devices. Their intention was to disrupt national holiday celebrations by detonating three bombs. This, they hoped, would get headlines for their cause, which was described on the report as 'Freedom for the indigenous Khmer peoples'.

It went on to explain that the group had done this kind of operation before and would give warnings ahead of time so people could be evacuated. This time they had said they were planning to hit a village and a temple and, while the Cambodian authorities were confident they could get the villagers out, the monks were proving more stubborn. Bombs or no bombs, the head of the Buddhist monks had decreed that his holy men would be staying in their wats, or temples, tending to their crops and observing their daily rituals.

The Faces were refusing to back down. And so was the Cambodian government.

It wasn't clear who had called in MeX, but the purpose of their mission was:

- Rendezvous at the Landing Zone (LZ)
- Proceed to the pre-programmed endpoint
- Find the Improvised Explosive Devices (IEDs) and trigger them without incurring casualties
- Remain undetected at all times

Jackson swung his way through more of MeXnet's classified documents, perusing maps and aerial photographs of jungle camps and temples that were straight out of *Tomb Raider*.

'And what are your thoughts, Farley?' Willard was glaring at him. 'Or are you too busy talking to yourself to talk to us?'

Jackson had been so immersed in what he was doing that he'd forgotten to disguise the commands he was using to work his way through the MeX research material.

'It's his imaginary friend!' Tyler Hughes rarely missed an opportunity to have a go.

'Sorry, Sir,' said Jackson, annoyed with himself for not being more vigilant. 'What was the question?

'I was asking for a description of a motte and bailey castle.'

Taking care to casually cover his mouth with a hand, Jackson silently enunciated SEARCH and was presented with MeXnet's own search-engine page. He then mouthed the words 'motte' and 'bailey'. The grommet instantly translated the nanoscale pressure shifts inside his ear, cross-checking them against an internal database of hundreds of thousands of words. A list of websites appeared over the faces of his class-mates. In a process that lasted all of a second, Jackson flexed the extra-ocular muscles of his right eye and opened the third link down belonging to a history Wiki.

'Motte is derived from the Norman-French word meaning "clod", "clump" or "hillock",' Jackson said, trying to sound casual and not give away the fact he was reading. 'The motte of a castle is a large mound, built using excavated earth, with a defensive ditch around its base. The bailey is the castle wall on top of the motte which contains the courtyard and surrounds the keep, the strongest part of the castle.'

'Yes . . . well . . . nice to have you back with us,' said Willard, surprised.

Relieved, Jackson tried not to grin. Being part of MeX was turning out to be one of the best things that had ever happened to him.

'Now we've heard from Jackson –' Willard turned his attention elsewhere – 'Mr Hughes, can you tell us what changes the Plantagenets brought to castle design?'

When Tyler couldn't answer, he threw Jackson a look as black as coal.

CHAPTER 13

'Good work today,' said Willard as Jackson followed the rest of the class down the corridor. 'See you at chess club – Monday night. We're gonna give this newfangled Bullet Chess a try!' he shouted, as he backed into the staffroom behind a leaning tower of textbooks.

Bullet Chess, thought Jackson as he walked towards the canteen. A whole game in just one minute. It was something he'd always wanted to try.

He was doubled over before he saw the duffel bag coming.

When he looked up, Jackson saw that he was surrounded. The group parted only to let their master in before closing back round him and Jackson like a hyena pack.

Tyler's face shared many of the features of a potato. His ginger hair was cropped so short as to be invisible, large ruddy blotches blighted his skin and one or two of his spots were as big and white as the sproutlings you get on spuds that are past their sell-by date. And this close up, he even smelled like something pulled from the dirt.

'It's the first sign, you know,' said Tyler, each word borne on a globule of spit.

'I'm . . . not sure I . . . follow you?' Jackson replied, trying to keep his voice from trembling.

'Talking to yourself – it's the first sign of madness.'

The underlings dissolved into laughter.

'Yes, well . . . I guess I must be mad.' Jackson saw Tyler's face instantly darken. The last thing he wanted to do was rub this oaf up the wrong way. But it was too late.

'You tryin' a be clever?' said Tyler, tightening his grip on the school tie that already threatened to garrotte Jackson.

There was no mistaking it, Jackson *was* clever. It wasn't like he flaunted it, but he was. Brilliant even. He was following a completely different arithmetic syllabus to the rest of the school and was expected to bypass sixth-form and go straight to university. He wasn't one of those little kids who wear bow ties and play the piano on chat shows when they're four, but, for a twelve-year-old, Jackson Farley was just plain, off-the-chart clever.

Jackson decided that the *clever* thing to do here was, unfortunately, to agree with everything his tormentor said – to apologize for whatever petty insecurity he'd triggered.

'Look, I'm sorry, OK. Please let me go?'

'*Please let me go*,' said Tyler in his best baby voice. 'Ah diddums – is Teacher's Pet scared?'

Jackson sighed. That plan obviously wasn't working. He was going to have to try something else. As Tyler turned to his minions to amuse them with his baby impersonation, Jackson mumbled his way into the school's computer. The home page flashed up over Tyler's guffawing face, then the STAFF AREA and the USERNAME and PASSWORD fields. Jackson mouthed 'Richard Willard', followed by 'Kasparov1985'.

He had known his history teacher's password for a while. When dealing with an amateur, and in terms of all things 'computer' that's what Mr Willard most certainly was, it was simply a case of finding out which of the world's most popular types of password applied to them. 'Password' consistently appeared as number 1 in a series of Top 100-style charts on the Web. The equally inane '123456' was a regular contender for the top spot, followed by a series of predictable inventions based around users' first names, pets, children and favourite sports teams. The combination of the godfather of chess and the year in which he became the youngest-ever world champion occurred to Jackson when he thought about how many times Willard had mentioned how he'd flown to Moscow with his uncle in 1985 to watch the 'most famous chess match in history'.

Jackson was into the Year 7 reports file and scanning the boys' section where he found Tyler's folder in seconds.

'Look! He's jabbering to himself again!' Tyler gibed. 'Perhaps he's a witch doctor! Voodoo's not gonna help you, I'm afraid,' he said, before landing a knee squarely in Jackson's privates. Suddenly the virtual display went blank, as Jackson was bent double, his MeX mobile phone clattering on to the concrete floor.

'What have we here?' said Tyler, bending to pick up the metallic handset with one hand, while holding Jackson by the scruff of the neck in the other. Tyler flipped the MeX phone, making the matt-silver clamshell do somersaults in the palm of his hand. 'Look what the little skinflint found in the bargain bucket.'

Jackson's heart sank. He needed to be near the handset for the rest of the MeX kit to work, so that he might avoid another serious kicking. He was going to have to do something. Ignoring the pain in his groin, he darted forward and grabbed at the aluminium handset as it completed another of Tyler's flips. The two boys grabbed hold of it at the same time, both trying to force it from the other's grip. Tyler pressed down hard on the bones in Jackson's arm. But the instant the handset made contact with Jackson's hand the electrons started to flow from its battery. They raced along the epidermis layer of his skin and shot up the cotton fibres of his shirt before energizing the very sinews of his neck and cheek, finding the tiny rivets on the grommet and infinitesimal contacts etched into the lens projector. A microsecond later and data began to flow again, the school website, the STAFF AREA holding page and Tyler's report popping up in a projection over the bull-headed boy's red face.

But Tyler still had his own grasp on the handset.

'Give me back my phone!' roared Jackson with a ferocity he didn't think he was capable of.

'Or you'll do what?' said Tyler, smirking.

Jackson wasn't proud of what he was about to do, but he didn't have any choice. He remembered when he'd wanted to let the remobot escape in the death-match. What was it Lear had said to him? *Hold our chins aloft and fight!*

Jackson found what he was looking for – a section in Tyler's file that detailed his father's conviction for 'Armed Burglary'. The paragraph went on to mention that, with no other parent, Tyler was in his grandmother's care.

'You what?' said Tyler, his voice cooling a little.

'I'll tell everyone where your dad is.'

Jackson felt sick at what he was saying – Tyler wasn't the only one with just one parent in this tussle – but it wasn't Jackson who was about to break someone's arm.

As Tyler relaxed his grip on Jackson's mangled tie and phone and slinked away with a mutter of 'You're not worth it', Jackson almost felt sorry for him.

CHAPTER 14

Jackson's muscles twinged painfully as he craned his neck to look at the wall of thousands of plump, forbidding folders on the tall shelves that surrounded him. He had chosen the census section of the local library to carry out his first-ever mission for MeX. It was somewhere he could expect a bit of privacy – after all, how many people would be spending their Saturday mornings reading census records on microfilm or county council minutes? Particularly not the likes of Tyler Hughes, Jackson thought, the memory of their last encounter making him shift, somewhat uncomfortably, in his chair.

Jackson had been woken by his MeX handset at 10 a.m. 'Mission commences in thirty minutes,' was all the characterless woman's voice had said. His dad would arrive home from his early-morning shift at any minute, and Jackson wasn't about to try and juggle his first mission with his dad's demands for a bacon sandwich or a pint of milk from the shop. He'd jumped out of bed, sprinted to the library and almost dropped the gooey contact lens projector trying to stick it in his eye.

The words 're-entry phase' blinked in his eye in shimmering red letters instantly. Jackson checked his handset – 10.55 a.m. – five minutes until the MeX unit burned through the Earth's atmosphere to its programmed location in Cambodia.

Jackson suddenly felt very nervous. In his rush to get to the library on time, he'd had some relief from the nerves that had been dogging him for the last couple of days, but now the butterflies were back. Jackson had studied the files and knew the mission profile back to front. But doing it for real was nothing like his evening sessions navigating the fantasy world of *Whisper*. Did he really have the abilities that Devlin Lear believed he had?

Jackson wondered if his three teammates were feeling the same. The twins had seemed unruffled by their first meeting with Lear. As for Brooke, if she had any doubts about her suitability for the job, she certainly didn't show them. Jackson had liked Brooke from the moment she'd first appeared in Lear's video chat. She said it like she saw it and she made him laugh.

His thoughts were snatched away as the library interior suddenly merged with the view fast-jet pilots must get when they fly swift and low.

The ten-centimetre biodegradable sphere that had kept

his MeX bot safe from temperatures hot enough to vaporize rock had been dropped, and the second-stage heat shield had folded itself out to form the triangular delta wing that would guide the bot in its final high-speed dash across an unbroken green canopy of Cambodian jungle. Finally, the robot saucer automatically ditched the delta wing and the automated launch system prepared to hand control over to Jackson.

The grey disc descended into its designated landing zone, a flat area of grassland ringed by a living wall of thick vegetation. The familiar woman's voice counted down: 'You have control in 5, 4, 3 . . .' By the time Jackson had command of his craft, it was hovering sedately a few metres above the ground.

'Well, that was a quick trip, but the lack of in-flight movies is unforgivable.' Unmistakably Brooke.

Jackson flicked his pen controller to one side, spinning his view round 180 degrees. The three dot.robots belonging to his teammates had assembled at the other side of the clearing.

Jackson took in as much of his surroundings as his live high-definition camera feed could offer. Even through the virtual medium of the Internet he could sense the life force of the jungle surrounding his machine. The clicks and chitters of insects and the high-pitched squawks of birds and monkeys were all around him. Jackson had read the material; he knew the tech that powered his tiny in-ear grommet. It was called 'Digital Sound Conduction'. The little grommet in his ear was using the framework of bones in his skull as a speaker, sending minuscule vibrations to set points around his head. It was like he was actually there, in the Cambodian jungle, every rustle of wind through the swaying trees, every screech and snake's slither filling his head and connecting him to the place.

'Time to lock and load,' said Brooke.

'Yeah. How we going to do this?' asked Jackson.

'You will lead us,' answered Miss Kojima.

Master Kojima's robot dipped its nose solemnly in what Jackson took to be the twin boy's approval. These highly skilled gamers were suggesting that he spearhead the mission.

Brooke confirmed the team's approval. 'You take the helm. You as skipper has worked for me so far.'

'OK, er . . . thank you,' said Jackson, trying not to show his surprise in his voice. The respect that the other recruits were showing in this decision was something that Jackson had never received from his peers at school. He brought up his spider's web display. A blinking end-point icon represented their destination, the village and temple deep in the jungle. There was an 'i' icon for information next to it, which opened automatically as Jackson's gaze fell on it, revealing some text:

```
Intel Update>>>
Suspect 3 IEDs:

• 2 devices in village
• 1 device in temple complex

Probable night-time
detonation.
```

'Well, we're looking at three bombs in two locations,'
Jackson began tentatively, looking at the faint outline
of a track on the map that led in the general direction
of the blinking endpoint. 'There's a trail to the right of
us. It leads into the jungle for about two kilometres
and should take us to the village. Let's go.'

He grasped his pen controller and tilted it gently
forward. Jackson's MeX$_1$ responded by gliding slowly
past the other three and towards a point at which the
lush tropical vegetation loomed above the landing zone.
Then he slotted his disc-shaped flying machine through
the only available gap in the nearly solid wall of greenery.
The other three bots followed.

It was dusk in this part of the world, but while the
sun had still been strong at the landing zone, it was
weak beneath the thick ceiling of trees. At first, the
downwash from the MeX$_1$ lift fans ripped up plumes
of damp leaves that sparkled in the streaks of sunlight

penetrating the thick foliage. But as they pressed on, deeper into the heart of the Angkorian forests, the tangle of branches and thick rubbery leaves began to choke even the sun's rays until the four machines might as well have been flying in the dead of night.

The going was slow as every few metres the trail would vanish, succumbing to a fallen tree with talon-like branches or a rubber plant with leaves as big as garage doors that the four virtual pilots needed to pick a route round. Eventually the trail disappeared completely; Jackson could still make out its outline, but there was only dense vegetation in front of his dot.robot. Twisted roots reared up towards them and Jackson had no choice but to lead the robotic convoy higher, guiding each machine between knotted branches and the limbs of palm trees. It was clear from the lack of communication that everyone was concentrating hard on just keeping up and avoiding being swatted by one of the massive wet rubbery fronds pushed aside by the machine in front of theirs. It was Brooke who broke the silence.

'OK, so now I understand how these Face dudes never seem to get caught. I can't see five metres in front of my machine.'

'You think they know we here?' asked Miss Kojima.

The thought had occurred to Jackson. At several points in the journey he'd noticed criss-crossing trees and bushes combining to make shapes that he imagined could have been a tattooed face or a man crouching in a tree top with a gun.

'This route to the temple was chosen so we wouldn't come into contact with anyone.' He said it as much for his own reassurance as that of his teammates. He took the quiet murmurs of agreement in his ear to mean it had worked for now anyway.

Eventually the foliage began to thin and Jackson was able to lead the bots back down to the jungle floor. The trail looked freshly cut, suggesting they were nearing some sort of development. In less than a kilometre he could see a clearing and some simple-looking buildings.

The village consisted of a sparse collection of huts, some on stilts, some made from a lattice of the same twisted wooden fingers that had barred the team's route through certain sections of the jungle. Others were just squares of crudely erected cinder blocks with corrugated-iron roofs. Several of the huts had open fronts with white plastic chairs and tables set out in front of them. Jackson thought they were probably the village shops. He saw that one building, little more than a lean-to made from a sheet of plastic and some poles, was sheltering a rusty barrel over which the charcoal-coloured carcass of some kind of animal was congealing. There were half-eaten plates of meat on the tables, with plastic knives and forks strewn across.

'I don't think much of the local Burger King,' said Brooke.

'Yeah, it looks like the customers left in a hurry,' said Jackson.

'Faces have village spooked good. There isn't even stray cat or dog!' Miss Kojima sounded a little spooked herself.

'That suits our purposes just fine,' Jackson replied. 'We know there are two bombs somewhere in this village and the other in the temple where the monks live. But for now we need to get rid of these two so the villagers can return to their homes.'

'Right then,' said Brooke. 'According to our mission notes, the explosives are simple little critters. The bomb-maker straps a battery and an alarm clock to whatever will give him the biggest bang for his buck. When the designated time is reached, the clock hands complete a circuit and the charge from the battery ignites the explosives. That's the theory anyway. The reality is they don't always go off. In order for the villagers to be given the all-clear to come home, we need to perform a controlled explosion of any device we can find.'

'Yeah, I read that too, but I still don't know how we're going to find them.'

'We no need find them. What is range of Dazzler?'

Jackson looked up in surprise at the first words Master Kojima had spoken on this mission.

'It's twenty-five metres.' Jackson never forgot a number.

'*Un!*' Miss Kojima's eyes lit up as she realized what her brother was suggesting. 'We spread out on your command. As long as in range, electric charge from Dazzlers should be enough to set off the bombs.'

A number-cruncher, two distinguished cyber athletes and a brilliant engineer. Perhaps Lear knew what he was doing. Jackson felt like everything might come together after all.

'One last thing. What if we're not close enough when we fire?' said Jackson. 'We've only got four Dazzlers between us.'

'I think this is one time we're going to have to rely on good ol' human judgement – it's up to us to decide what looks like a possible target.'

Brooke's machine was hovering at the edge of the town square by a rusty old tuk-tuk, a type of motorcycle with a cabin attached to the rear that local people used as a taxi. It was top of the list on Jackson's mental list of bomb targets.

'OK, Brooke, on my command,' said Jackson. '5, 4, 3, 2, 1. Go!'

The Dazzler lit up the shadowy village in an instant, its electric-blue glare searing the silhouette of the huts deep into Jackson's retina and causing his right eye to water. It took a few seconds before he could see clearly enough to notice that the tuk-tuk motorcycle had vanished.

'It . . . land . . . behind Burger King!' said Miss Kojima.

'Home run!' shouted Brooke, her remobot untouched by the blast.

'OK, I'll go next. Wearing my bomber's cap, I'd say that pigsty, or whatever it is, at the other edge of the village looks suspect,' said Jackson.

He was looking at a squat structure made of reed matting and sheets of corrugated metal. Its bamboo gate hung open on frayed rope hinges and he could see the floor inside was a mixture of mud and straw. It made sense that the inhabitants of the village would have taken their precious livestock with them when they received orders to evacuate.

'Pardon me . . . but I think . . . bomb in . . . gas . . . station.' It was the voice of Master Kojima. Jackson had seldom heard him speak. Almost all communications with the Kojimas were handled by his sister, probably because she was the most fluent speaker. 'I try?' asked the Japanese boy.

'Be my guest,' replied Jackson. He hadn't realized that the lean-to, filled with plastic bottles, was in fact the village petrol station, but had to agree that – as potential bomb locations went – it seemed like a good candidate.

Master Kojima's MeX$_1$ drifted down the street, coming to a stop halfway down, several shelters up from the gas station.

'5, 4, 3, 2, 1. Go!' cried Jackson.

Once again, the detonation of the Dazzler hurt to look at, but given that all four recruits were viewing the flash via Retinal Projectors, there was no way of avoiding its intense glare.

This time, however, there was no explosion. As Jackson's vision returned to normal he could see that the lean-to was perfectly intact.

'Doh! You missed,' said Brooke, displaying her usual tact.

'I . . . sorry,' said Master Kojima, the disappointment obvious in his voice. 'I shame team.'

'Don't worry about it,' said Jackson. 'We have other options.' Jackson wasn't sure what exactly those options were, given that they were now two Dazzlers down, but he could tell how guilty his Japanese teammate was feeling and didn't want to make him feel any worse.

A few minutes later, Miss Kojima fired her Dazzler on Jackson's cue, and the four dot.robots moved off towards the temple complex, leaving the burning shell of the pigsty behind them.

Two bombs down. One to go.

CHAPTER 15

The temple complex was a stately collection of old stone buildings huddled together and topped with a jumble of roofs organized in layers. From where the MeX machines were hovering, the slate roofs, edged with wood and gilt, formed shapes against the jungle backdrop like a flotilla of ships on a big green sea.

'We've only got one more explosive device to find, but just one Dazzler, so we need to decide carefully where our target is. Brooke, I think you and Master Kojima should scout out the temple itself first and locate the monks.'

'Hey, boy wonder, you up for this?' said Brooke.

'*Un*,' replied the downcast Japanese boy, still obviously disappointed at his previous mistake.

Jackson watched the two saucers move off, each hugging the base of the ancient wall that surrounded the enclosure before they edged round an archway and slipped inside. The wall was alive with the stone faces of fierce-looking animals and dancing natives; its four sides constituted a huge stone tapestry that depicted everything the people of this place had loved, feared and worshipped for thousands of years. The sun had already sunk behind the temple skyline and Jackson guessed it would be dark in about twenty minutes. Based on The Faces' previous record, once night-time set in it was only a matter of time before their remaining device exploded. He felt the familiar pangs of uncertainty in his stomach. The village might have been deserted, but the temple held no such guarantee. The monks could be anywhere. And it wasn't just the bomb that was cause for concern; the Dazzler and the Bass Bomb might have been non-lethal, but they could still inflict serious harm on someone. Everything had to go to plan.

Master Kojima was waiting for Brooke. They'd decided that she would do a circuit of the temple corridors to sniff out its inhabitants and he would wait to see if she stirred anything up. He was good at waiting. He had once told a journalist from a Japanese gaming magazine that *waiting* was the one ingredient he expected to find missing from most of his adversaries' game play. They would bounce around the game map, blasting all of the usual hiding places with their rocket-propelled grenades, giving away their position with every shot, every grunt and every footfall; while all he did was wait, quietly.

It wasn't long before his patience paid off and a lone monk strolled across the courtyard in front of the cubby-hole he'd found for his remobot. The man wore a bright orange robe and had his head buried in a large leather-bound book.

'I see . . . monk,' reported Master Kojima.

'What about you, Brooke?' Jackson checked.

'I'm staring at monks, mission control!'

Brooke was looking through a window into a large hall where ten or so figures sat round a large wooden table. Three others were pouring them water from a wooden pitcher. Each had a shaven head and a single piece of bright orange loose-flowing fabric tied at their shoulders. They looked like clones.

'OK, so we know they share a weakness for orange. What more do we need to find out?'

Jackson observed the blinking icons in the inner circle of his spider display and could see that the hall Brooke was referring to was on the east side of the complex, right next to the main gate that led out to the jungle road.

'Did you see anyone else on your travels?'

'Nada! This is the only party in town!'

'OK, guys, listen carefully . . .'

Jackson's plan was simple. Brooke's MeX_1 would herd the men out of the hall and through the main exit. Master Kojima would do the same with the sole remaining monk.

Miss Kojima would give the signal when they were safely outside. Then Jackson would fly his machine into position inside the compound to detonate the bomb with his remaining Dazzler.

'Does this mean I get to use the HAIL function?' asked Brooke.

'Whatever gets the job done,' said Jackson.

The reference to HAIL was buried deep in the MeX manual:

> **HAIL.** The MeX$_1$ has the ability to capture sounds from the microphone located in the user's in-ear Stealth Communicator for real-time 'playback' via a single acoustic fabric speaker system.
> **BE ADVISED!**
> Use of HAIL is strongly discouraged as it may lead to a contravention of Section 1.3, Clause 4 of the International Stealth Agreement.

The screeching of the young American's HAIL reverberated around the temple corridors like the howls of a banshee. When she was at full wail, Brooke flew her robot at the hall window, filling the room with fragments of glass and ear-splitting sound. Her saucer-shaped machine skimmed low over the wooden table around which most of the orange-clad men sat, toppling pitchers and slinging clay pots and mugs on to the stone floor. She then banked the dot.robot high into the hall's vaulted ceiling and brought it to a hover before letting loose an even shriller cry that was pitched so high Jackson thought the grommet in his ear had grown teeth and bitten him.

Brooke surveyed the hall below her MeX$_1$, expecting to see the men raising up their robes and running for the doorway to get out. But far from fleeing, to her amazement, the holy men had dropped to their knees and begun to chant.

'They ain't leavin', but at least they're all in one place. This ol' hall is as full as a fat lady's sock!' Brooke said hoarsely.

'Let's just hope the third explosive device isn't in your hall,' replied Jackson cautiously.

At the other side of the complex, Master Kojima had followed the lone monk to a statue at the centre of a small courtyard. He watched as the monk, who had been absorbed in his book the whole time, knelt before the statue and placed his book on the ground. He expected to see him start praying, but instead he began to rummage underneath the red material that shrouded the stone figure and gathered at its feet. Master Kojima pushed his MeX$_1$ forward, hugging the edge of the courtyard until the machine came to a collection of big palms in pots. He carefully pushed the camera lens on the front of his machine between the fan-shaped leaves until he could clearly see the monk's face from sideways on.

There wasn't a centimetre of the shaven-headed man's face that wasn't tattooed. The indelible ink body of a snake was coiled round his neck, rising to a fanged head that threatened to leap from his cheek. His ears and mouth were garlanded with strange symbols and the image of the clawed foot and scaly body of some mythical creature clung to the top of his head. This was one of The Faces.

Then Master Kojima noticed that he was holding something that looked like a shoe box. As the tattooed fighter carefully lifted the lid, the Japanese boy could just make out an old-fashioned alarm clock inside, the kind with two polished bells on top. Coils of red-and-black wire connected the clock to a sealed steel cylinder. The man quickly checked the contents of the box and, after fixing the lid back in place, slid it carefully back under the red shroud.

'Bomb!' shouted Master Kojima. 'I see . . . bomb!'

Jackson listened as both Kojima twins started to babble furiously in Japanese, then the young girl spoke to him.

'My brother say he see one of Faces. He think he speed up bomb!'

'You won't wanna hear this either,' said Brooke. 'I

may have overdone the scare tactics! Two of my monks just ran back into the temple. I'm not sure, but they could be heading in Master Kojima's direction.'

Jackson felt his pulse begin to race. He had to detonate the bomb before the two panic-stricken monks wandered into its path.

As Miss Kojima set off to try and find the runaway monks, Jackson snapped the nose of his dot.robot downwards. With the flying disc almost vertical to the ground, the blades of its ducted fan engine ripped through the air and hurled it along the aisles of the ancient temple, weaving through the hallways, trees and jungle plants that grew inside as well as out.

The tattooed man had almost reached the cluster of plants where Master Kojima's remobot was hiding when Jackson's machine screamed into the open courtyard. The jungle fighter was quick to react, rolling across the cobblestone floor and rising to a kneeling position, his gun pointing directly at Jackson's machine.

Master Kojima made his move. The MeX_1 shot through the foliage, arriving between the tattooed fighter and Jackson's machine as two bullets left the hand-gun's barrel. The supersonic slugs pounded into the thin thermoplastic outer shell of Master Kojima's machine, the spike of pressure ripping off a fist-sized chunk of battery and carrying it clean through one of the processors responsible for the remobot's fly-by-wire controls.

The robotic disc pranged off one of the stone pillars that supported the cloister, leaving Master Kojima powerless to stop his machine from slamming into the wall.

Miss Kojima was a couple of corridors away from the glowing icons that represented Jackson and her brother when she spotted the two monks. 'Two orange men . . . coming to you.'

'Detonate . . . now!' shouted Master Kojima. But the jungle fighter had switched his attention to Jackson's machine, which the twelve-year-old had just managed to reverse into the cluster of plants in an attempt to avoid being shot.

'I can't see the target!' shouted Jackson. 'I need to be sure it's within range.'

The tattooed man had his back to the downed grey disc controlled by Master Kojima when he heard its engine spool up. He immediately stopped and spun round into a steady firing stance. He knew he'd hit it with his first volley, but he wasn't about to take any chances. For all his readiness, as the mysterious machine's engine roared, the disc that had seemed so nimble in the air just skipped erratically about the pebbles, dashing its damaged fuselage against the walls and pillars. The seasoned jungle fighter, who had been sent by his commander to check that their third and final incendiary device was still intact, after the two they'd set in the village had apparently malfunctioned, could see that the machine was broken. After he'd put another couple of rounds into it and downed the one in the palms, he thought, he would pick them up and take them back to camp. *When will the Americans learn that their technology is no match for the jungle fighters of Cambodia?*

He was taking aim when, in the corner of his eye, he caught the shape of Jackson's machine breaking cover. But by then it was too late. A third machine came out of nowhere. Miss Kojima's dot.robot hit the tattooed man squarely in the stomach, the momentum of the strike bending him double and carrying him backwards through the covered entrance to the courtyard.

'Now, Jackson!' shouted Master Kojima.

The harsh light from Jackson's Dazzler seared into the back of his eyeball. There was no getting used to it. At the same time his view was shaken, as a wave of hot air from the courtyard explosion washed over his machine.

Miss Kojima's MeX_1 was scorched but otherwise undamaged; the stone archway above her robotic craft had absorbed the brunt of the fiery force that had burst from the statue. A few metres away from her lay the tattooed man. For a moment she feared he might be dead, but then, slowly, he rose from the stone floor that he had tried shamelessly to meld with as the superheated flames roared overhead.

The man turned, brushing ash and the fragments of

smouldering ferns and palm leaves from his clothes, and stared with clear, bright eyes ringed with hand-drawn thorns at the machine that he now realized had saved him from the ravages of his own bomb.

He then about-faced and sprinted away.

CHAPTER 16

Jackson felt great. In the week that followed the successful jungle mission, the four recruits had been called upon to escort a shipment of food aid along a lawless stretch of the Somali Peninsula and guard a warehouse full of computers intended for African schools, which rebels had threatened to steal. Following each mission, Lear had sent them each a video message comprising a quick debrief and a heads-up about their next assignment. They were then given access to the relevant MeXnet files, which they were expected to study diligently.

The missions were exhausting and Jackson had school and homework to keep up with, but the feeling of hitting criminals where it hurt was intoxicating. Lear's praise, which was often lavished on Jackson in particular, made him feel like he counted for something and, if Jackson had had any doubts about MeX before, they'd been washed away in the swell of the most exciting week of his life.

He had spent the previous two evenings – and a good

deal of his school breaks and bus rides – immersed in the details of the team's next mission which was scheduled to take place in Ukraine. Lear had described it as a simple reconnaissance job. 'Don't expect the thrills and spills of your jungle adventure,' he'd said. 'This is a simple point-and-click affair. Think of yourselves as invisible tourists. Just turn up, take some snaps and disappear.'

The background of the East European assignment, which focused on a Ukrainian gangland figure known as General Dragos, fascinated Jackson. According to the intelligence report, Yuri Stanislav Dragos was an ex-military commander turned businessman grown rich during the Russian oil boom. His sights were now set on getting a piece of the planet's hottest commodity – water. It was alleged that Dragos was using a private security force to flatten a path through villages and farms in Ukraine's Ural mountain region – forcing landowners to leave their homes for a supposed property development scheme when, according to MeX, he was actually laying a secret underground pipe network to drain the region of its natural water reserves. According to information on MeX's intranet, clean drinking water was increasingly hard to come by and companies worldwide were lining up to control what the citizens of certain countries drank. If someone like Dragos was able to control the water that people desperately needed, he could charge massive prices and make huge profits.

Jackson was confident that he'd read all the relevant material supplied by MeX. He'd even swotted up on Ukraine and the countries that bordered it from material he'd sourced online. Whenever the call from MeX came, he would be ready. He just hoped it wouldn't be tonight. It was Friday night and Brooke had suggested the team members meet online for a chat.

He squeezed a narrow sausage of mayonnaise on to the thin slice of ham in his sandwich that formed the peak of a precariously balanced food tower consisting of sandwich, cold pizza, several chocolate bars and a yoghurt on top. He was hoping to make his way quietly to his room when Mr Farley came straight out of the lounge and almost walked into him.

'You're being suspiciously quiet,' said Mr Farley.

'That's because I'm performing secret experiments in my room, Dad,' replied Jackson, steadying the pile he was carrying by placing his chin on top of the yoghurt.

'Experiments that require most of the contents of the fridge?' It was true that Jackson had depleted the fridge of a good deal of its contents over the course of the week in order to support his late-night sessions. 'Don't worry about it,' his dad continued. 'Food's there to be eaten. Don't suppose you want to curl up on the sofa? There's a movie about to start.'

'Thanks, Dad, but I've just finished my homework so I can play *Whisper*.' Jackson had no intention of playing his favourite game, but saying its name made him realize how strange it was that something he had played almost every day for a whole year could feel like the distant past after a break of just a few days.

'I hate to say it, son, but I'd like to think there was something more constructive you could do with that brain of yours.'

Jackson wished he could tell his dad about MeX. He'd imagined himself telling his dad how he, out of all the possible candidates in the country, the world even, had been chosen; about the people he and his three new friends had already helped. And he'd already thought about sitting him down on the sofa and taking him through the MeX gear. His dad loved reading about all the new gadgets in the Sunday newspapers, and the grommet and in-eye projector would have astonished him. But he would also have been freaked out by the whole thing. He would have wanted to know who MeX were and why they were contacting children without asking for their parents' permission. But, worst of all, he probably would have stopped him. Anyway, thought Jackson, he and the others were sworn to secrecy.

'Dad. Relax. It's Friday night. And if I don't get this food out from under my chin soon, there's a danger I'm going to stay like this.' He had been bent forward like an old man for the entire conversation, trying to keep the Leaning Tower of Foodstuffs from taking a spill on to the carpet. As he moved off towards his bedroom, his father called after him.

'You know we're only a few days away from Mum's special day. You still good to get the sunflowers?'

Jackson hadn't forgotten the anniversary of his mother's death. 'I'm good.'

Then both of them disappeared behind their respective doors.

As Jackson settled down in front of his computer, he could see that Brooke was already online. She accepted his request for a video chat.

'I think he's cute,' said Brooke. She was looking off camera at something on her computer screen.

'Who's cute?' Jackson asked.

'Dragos. He has a kind of film star thing going on.'

'If you're talking about the MeXnet mugshot of him, I think he looks like a scumbag,' said Jackson. There were several long-lens snaps of the man in the classified documents which the team had all been given access to. It wasn't the face Jackson had in mind for such a dangerous man. An eye patch or a scar wouldn't have gone amiss. Dragos had a lion's mane of shiny, jet-black hair that framed finely chiselled features. But his eyes were fiery beneath the thick black eyebrows and in all the photographs he wore the same black beret, which, to Jackson at least, meant he wasn't afraid to use his old military muscle to back up his business deals.

'It's a shame we're only allowed to use our camera on him,' he said.

'Check out Rambo,' Brooke said, smiling. 'A few missions under his belt and he thinks he's got a licence to kill.'

'What about those pictures of the forests and farms he's dug up for his pipeline?' Jackson was referring to satellite images on MeXnet. Because of the mountainous terrain, MeX had been unable to get clear enough images of what were described as Dragos's 'slash-and-burn' tactics. Although the pixellated images were shocking enough, according to their briefing material their first proper mission was to get in close and capture some clearer photographic and video evidence.

'You're right . . . he's a good-looking scumbag,' said Brooke.

Jackson's computer emitted a soft harp sound and a small box with the word 'Kojima' popped up. After he had accepted the twins' request to join the video chat, a window containing the Japanese duo materialized, next to the one showing Brooke.

'Good . . . morning . . . teammates,' said Miss Kojima, both twins adding their by now habitual bow, to which Jackson and Brooke felt compelled to respond with their own shallow dips of the head.

'It's night-time here,' replied Jackson. 'But I get your meaning.'

'For us . . . sun just rise. We no stay long.'

Brooke grinned. 'We know, honey. You gotta keep Daddy happy. We're just glad you could both make it.'

The twins had shared details of their gruelling daily routine with Jackson and Brooke as the recruits got to know each other during their recent missions. Physical exercise at the crack of dawn, then schooling and game practice right up until bedtime.

'There's something I've been meaning to ask you guys,' said Brooke. 'What's with the Master and Miss? Y'all go by any other names?'

'Yes. We just no use them,' replied Miss Kojima.

Her brother tugged on her arm and they whispered for a moment before she turned back to the webcam.

'If you want . . . we tell you.'

Brooke thought for a second before she said, 'D'you know what? Come to think about it, I reckon I'd prefer you kept 'em mysterious.'

Jackson agreed.

'We have question also . . . for Jackson,' said Miss Kojima. 'Have you met . . . the Queen?'

Brooke laughed. 'I've been meaning to ask the same thing.'

Jackson considered the question before answering. 'Yes, of course. Her Majesty lives near me, here in

Peckham. We see her all the time.' It wasn't all lies, not completely. He had once been in a crowd, waving a Union Jack, when a car containing the Queen sped past. 'In fact my bedroom window is directly opposite Buckingham Palace. I can see it from where I'm sitting.' Now he was flat-out fibbing.

'Shoot – you're kidding, right?' said Brooke.

'No, really, I can,' said Jackson, swivelling his webcam round towards his bedroom window.

It was dark outside, but because the Farleys' flat was so high up there was a good view of the city.

Brooke and Miss Kojima waited for the image from Jackson's webcam to clear as the pixels settled. Soon the feed from the camera showed a latticework of dimly lit windows.

'Omigod!' said the young American. 'Is that really Queen Elizabeth's house?'

The Kojimas were both visibly excited by the blotchy image they were being fed.

'Yes . . . the whole penthouse is her bedroom,' said Jackson, using his finger to point out a row of four glowing squares on the top floor of what was actually the block of flats directly opposite his.

'I'm kidding, by the way,' Jackson added.

'We know you are,' said Brooke nonchalantly.

'Yes. British humour . . . world famous,' said Miss Kojima.

The four of them laughed.

'My brother just got screen-shot of your . . . fake . . . Buckingham Palace,' Miss Kojima continued. 'We show father. He will think our new English gamer friend is . . . royal prince.'

The four of them burst out laughing again.

'So that's how you're able to keep up with MeX commitments?' asked Jackson, thinking about the movie invitation he'd just turned down from his dad.

'Yes. Father think it good we meet and play with international gamers.'

The young Japanese girl explained how her father had plans to send her and her brother on a world game-playing tour. And while Jackson still found the lives of his new superstar gaming friends amazing, he didn't envy them. Eventually the twins' attention was taken by the presence of what Jackson guessed was their father in the room. He heard a few staccato Japanese phrases off-camera and then the twins bowed politely and Miss Kojima said goodbye. Her brother winked at the camera, leaned forward and disconnected.

'Gee, I don't envy those two,' said Brooke.

'I know what you mean,' Jackson replied. 'But I'd still rather be doing what they're doing than be stuck in some dead-end school.'

'Sounds to me like you're talking from experience.'

Jackson hesitated. Though it had never been a great

experience, thanks to the likes of Tyler Hughes, Jackson realized even the classes he'd previously enjoyed had taken a backseat to his MeX missions. 'Maybe,' he replied.

'I figured you'd get to go to a special school, what with you being a genius and all.'

'Genius?' Jackson stuttered. 'Whatever gave you that idea?'

'Your blog!'

Jackson had set up *math-fu.com* on a whim, as a way of testing his web-coding skills. But it had developed into a regular meeting post for the mathematically curious. Mostly it consisted of random comments and questions that visitors would bat back and forth for weeks; things like 'How much would it cost to cover the Earth in chocolate spread?' (Most answers hovered around the figure £216,080,000,000,000 and were based on an agreed price of £1.46 per square metre and a total land surface of 148,327,070 square kilometres.) Jackson had also posted examples of his favourite 'workings-out' and a few photographs of mathematical origami models, including his first-ever model, a stack of three Columbus Cubes – a simple variation of the basic paper cube with a dent in one corner that meant several could be stacked on top of each other. He was most proud of his Photoshopped profile picture – a barely recognizable Jackson, dressed as a ninja.

'GallifreyGirl thinks you're a *genius*,' said Brooke. Her face was illuminated as she brought up Jackson's page on her monitor.

The fellow *Dr Who* fan had bestowed the compliment on Jackson when he'd answered a question she'd posted about Happy Prime Numbers. He was familiar with the episode that had GallifreyGirl stumped, in which the Timelord had to guess the next number in a sequence of Happy Primes in order to unlock a door. The Doctor had gone on to give a rather garbled explanation of Happy Prime Numbers to his crew – an explanation that had left GallifreyGirl most vexed.

'How to tell if your prime number is HAPPY!!!' began Jackson's reply.

Choose your prime number (any number which is only divisible by 1 and itself), say 23. To find out if it's 'happy' or not, all you do is break it down to its digits – so 2 and 3. Now it's just a matter of squaring and adding until you arrive at a single digit. If you can get to the magic number 1 – then the 23 you started with is happy! Get it?

Let's see if the prime number 23 is happy or not:

First up – separate the digits: 2 & 3

Square each digit and find the sum of the results:
2x2 + 3x3

That makes 4 + 9 = 13

Just keep separating the digits, then 'squaring and adding':

$1\times1 + 3\times3$ (that's $1 + 9$) $= 10$

$1\times1 + 0\times0 = 1$

So 23 <u>is</u> a Happy Prime (just like '379' which the good Doctor used to open the door!!!)

P.S. My favourite prime number (271097) is both happy and sad. Happy because it's my birthday (27 October 1997)! Sad because it's not a 'happy prime' – if that makes any sense :-/

'See, your birthday's a prime number! That could only happen to a genius,' said Brooke, wrestling with a spoon and a gargantuan tub of ice cream. 'Oh . . . and I dig the poetics, by the way,' she blurted through a mouthful. She'd spotted the Pi poem, which Jackson had placed at the top of his page. It could have been treated like a sacred artefact, hidden in the bottom of a drawer or framed and gathering dust, but that's not what his mum would have wanted. She was the outgoing member of the family, the one who Jackson and his dad pretended was embarrassing at parties, and so it was only fitting that Jackson put her poem on the Web where everyone and anyone could read it. Whether they'd understand it was another matter.

Brooke listened, spellbound as Jackson revealed the

secret behind his mother's six-line legacy. He failed to mention anything about the car crash that had taken her away. He found it impossible to talk about that even now and – thankfully – Brooke was too polite to ask.

'Gee, my mom couldn't write a shopping list! But then she can strip out a gear box in a minute flat.'

'Is that why you're so useful with a spanner?'

'Poppa's the brains; Momma's the muscle.'

'What is it precisely that you do? Is it true you've already graduated from uni?'

'Straight As at the age of eleven . . . although it's gotta help when your dad is head of faculty. Not that we've seen much of the campus of late – we're working flat out on Poppa's latest project, see.'

'Which is?'

'Asteroid robotics.'

'No two ways about it, the mining of near-Earth aster-oids is where it's at,' said Brooke, referring to an artist's impression of a bright yellow robot clinging to the side of a pockmarked chunk of space rock which she'd file-transferred over to Jackson. 'Nickel, iron, platinum . . . they've got 'em by the bucketload. There's a cosmic gold rush out there just waiting for some robot roughnecks to come and dig up the booty and haul it back home.'

'And this is what you're building?' Jackson asked, looking at the comic-book-style mining droid, whose spindly little robot hands were having trouble holding on to the asteroid as it hurtled through space.

'Heck, no!' said Brooke, poking at keys. 'Try this . . .'

A file-transfer request appeared on Jackson's monitor. The image that eventually loaded was of something that wouldn't have looked out of place in a medieval knights' weapons cache. It was a perfectly round silver ball, made up of several rectangular sections of metal that were roughly riveted and welded together. Jackson could tell it was the size of a large beach ball because Brooke was leaning into the shot – grinning.

'We've got a few designs, but this is my favourite,' said Brooke. 'I call him *Punk*.'

'OK . . .'

'Oh, come on . . . you're a Brit! Don't tell me you don't see haircuts like his every day on the streets of London?'

'Oh . . . er . . . sure I do,' said Jackson, not wanting to disappoint. Now he came to think of it, before Amisha Patel had gone exclusively goth, she had been through a punk-rock stage, during which she'd come to school with a series of geometrically perfect cones kept in gravity-defying gelled suspension all over her head. Amisha's crusty structures were indeed very similar to the sinister-looking spikes all over *Punk*'s surface.

'And your dad's gonna send . . . *Punk* . . . into space?'

'Yes and no. Right now we're working with demo

rigs, designed to be sent up into low Earth orbit – about three hundred kilometres up – then back down to work on terrestrial desert rocks.'

'And where do you come in?'

'Chief Engineer and Test Pilot,' she said, saluting the webcam. 'Pops likes to keep things in the family. The bots are mainly automated, but I get hands-on if something flash needs doin'.'

'So there's more besides . . . *Punk*?'

'You betcha . . . when you're trying to get a Chinese CEO to part with a hundred million bucks – it pays to keep the pantry well stocked!'

The American's life was a world apart from Jackson's own humdrum existence. Flying space robots? He was lucky if his dad let him borrow his racing bike to get groceries, he was so stingy with his stuff.

'This is my real baby, though,' said Brooke, interrupting Jackson's thoughts and scooping up her webcam to point it, hand-held, into the room behind her. The slightly wonky view Jackson was offered showed a substantial workroom, with a deep ruby-red Hummer off-roader parked in the middle.

'Hold on – you keep a Hummer in your bedroom?' Jackson couldn't believe what he was seeing.

'Nope.' Brooke didn't even bat an eyelid. 'I keep a bed in my garage.'

*

'So the car drives itself?' Jackson asked eagerly.

'In theory . . . yes,' replied Brooke. She had spent the last ten minutes explaining all about the X-Challenge desert race and the robotic car she'd spent every morsel of her precious little spare time building. She'd even shown him a video that she and her dad had put together and uploaded on to YouTube.

It opened with a silhouette hunched in the centre of a fountain of sparks from a welding torch. As the sparks subsided, the welder pulled up her visor and it became clear it was the eccentric pink-haired American. 'Hi, I'm Brooke English,' she said, the shot widening to reveal the Hummer H3R beside her. 'And this is *Tin Lizzie*, my entry for the X-Challenge.' The film cut to a series of shots of the outlandish vehicle, looking like a warthog with exotic devices protruding from its roof. It raced across desert and dirt tracks and performed a series of impressive jumps and skids, all without a driver onboard, concluding with a nimble 180 that threw a cloud of dirt over an unfazed Brooke.

'Sorry 'bout the music,' said Brooke, referring to the film's out-of-place soundtrack. 'Pops insisted on playin' along with his darned organ. You can rev her up if you like.'

Jackson wasn't sure which revelation was the most unexpected – the fact that a world-renowned robotics professor with his own space program could play the organ quite so badly – or that Brooke had just offered to let him rev a car that was in a garage 8,000 kilometres away.

'How's it work then?' asked a very excited Jackson. 'TCP/IP, baby!'

Transmission Control Protocol/Internet Protocol or TCP/IP was the shared language of the Internet – the way in which all web-connected devices talk to each other. As far as Jackson was concerned, it was basic computer-class stuff. But using the Net to remotely control a two-tonne monster-truck – that was something he didn't get to do in class.

'When the Challenge goes down, *Lizzie* will do all the driving herself, but while we iron out some of the quirks of her personality, it's safer if I'm at the controls,' said Brooke, back to punching keys. 'We had real problems with our radio signals in certain parts of the desert, but our cell phones always seemed to work. So I suggested we use one of them as an Internet data link!'

A hyperlink arrived in Jackson's Messenger window, which led to a web page on which a number of rudimentary computer graphics were laid over a large video feed from behind the Hummer's steering wheel.

'Here . . . I'll send you the keys!' said Brooke.

'GeekSugar' and 'UWillNev3rGuess' appeared in his Messenger mail and Jackson dutifully copied them into the page's username and password fields. As he stabbed the ENTER key, the view juddered and he could hear the throaty snarl of an engine starting up.

'Feel free to gun the throttle slider!' said Brooke, raising her voice as the dark red vehicle purred away behind her.

Jackson moved his mouse pointer over a cluster of graphical readouts: a gear-shifter showing DRIVE, REVERSE, NEUTRAL, FIRST and SECOND, a large red button labelled AUTO-DRIVE and a THROTTLE slider. He nudged the slider upwards until it read '80%'. Even over his tinny headphones the noise was impressive.

'Would ya . . . listen to that?' yelled Brooke, the roar from the SUV threatening to swallow her words. 'Six cylinders of road-hoggin' robot!'

Jackson grinned. He could have listened to the sound all night.

CHAPTER 17

Jackson received the call at 5 a.m., three hours after he and Brooke had punched out. Two hours after he'd managed to lull his head, jam-packed with asteroids and full-sized remote-control cars, to sleep. He was sitting by his computer, which was showing some information about General Dragos he'd managed to dredge up himself from the Web while the MeX lens in his right eye was telling him he had just three minutes to go before touchdown. It stung. That was something he hadn't got used to. Everything else – the repetition of the mission-briefing material in his mind, the nervous way he twisted and flicked the MeX fountain pen in his hand in anticipation of the moment when it would become a finely tuned robot control stick – they were all familiar by now.

A screen popped up over the words projected into his retina. It read 'Incoming Video Message'. A moment later Jackson was looking at the face of Devlin Lear.

'Hello, team,' Lear began. 'Your performance on the

missions so far has been outstanding. Today should be a walk in the park. I'm interested in anything you can film, photograph and otherwise record of this wretched thief, Dragos. And that's it.' Lear flicked his flaxen hair to one side and moved closer to the camera that was recording him. 'Remember,' he continued, his voice lowered to a whisper. 'Be the eyes and ears, my friends, but not the mouth – for the mouth doth betray itself.' And with that, the video transmission ended.

Lear's performance put Jackson in mind of an old hammy actor. It might have been a little theatrical, but he admired what Lear stood for. Here was a billionaire, with a string of international businesses to run, and yet he cared so much about putting a stop to the villainous actions of men like General Dragos that he had willed MeX into being and was intimately connected with every mission. Jackson hoped that Lear could see that he felt the same. He certainly intended to do everything in his power today to help put Dragos behind bars.

'Touchdown in 5, 4, 3, 2 . . .' The voice of MeXnet announced his machine's arrival and seconds later the four dot.robots were hugging the contours of the weather-beaten Ukrainian countryside.

'Nap of the Earth, sugar!' said Brooke. 'It's the only way to fly.'

The four small robots flew low, keeping the pines and the lakes and the quaint little hamlets and tumbledown farmhouses within arm's reach, veiling themselves in the valleys and the bristle of thickets just enough to keep them safe from detection by radar. Jackson guided the team along the belly of a gully strewn with drizzle-kissed claystone boulders that glistened like snake scales, then out over miles of flatland where they stalked the copses that dotted the landscape, leaving a flurry of copper-coloured leaves in their wake. It was as if the whole country was asleep under a thick blanket, the shrouded fans on the four machines picking at the mist in wisps.

While none of the young MeX pilots knew exactly what to expect when they neared the blinking waypoint on their displays, Jackson secretly hoped it would involve catching the rogue general with the oil-black hair red-handed. But as they slowed the dot.robots to a hover at the edge of a slim cluster of beech trees, his mind was on something else. It was a feeling that had dogged him for most of the journey, the feeling that someone – or something – was following them.

It was an eerie sensation, that through all the hard-ware, the noughts and ones that networked their way across his skin, the silicon and radio waves and the fibre-optic jungle of the Internet, he could still sense they were being shadowed.

'Did you see that?' Jackson's senses were on high alert.

'What?' replied Brooke.

'It's probably nothing . . . there was a blip on my map . . . lasted a second is all . . . then it was gone.'

The MeX$_1$s' spider displays were configured to show only certain types of objects: fast-jets and helicopters, troop carriers and tanks, the distinctive shape a man makes when he's holding a Kalashnikov – it was important to recognize these things so they could be avoided.

'We saw it too,' said Miss Kojima. 'We no worry . . . innocent aeroplane.'

'You're right,' said Jackson. The tension of this latest mission was getting to him. 'Let's keep going.'

There had been blips and flashes on his spider display before and he'd ignored them all. That's what happens when you throw electromagnetic waves around, he thought; they aren't selective about which surfaces they bounce off – pylons, car bonnets, even rainclouds – anything could register for a millisecond or two.

Soon the glistening landscape ebbed away and the robot convoy was surrounded on both sides by banks of freshly excavated soil. It wasn't until Jackson had nodded his MeX$_1$ under the third in a series of concrete bridges that he realized they were following the rocky spine of a riverbed. At one time, it must have been a major waterway, judging by the size of the concrete bridges that straddled it. Now little more than a stream meandered its way across the boulders and piles of rubble.

They tacked northwards, pulling their craft up and

over the lofty mudbanks that had shielded them from the worst of the rain. As Jackson crested the sludgy embankment, through the wall of silver needles thrown from sudden heavy rainclouds he saw the source of all the debris.

'Wowzer,' said Brooke. 'It's like the whole village fell into the river.'

Or was pushed, thought Jackson. He looked at the topographical overlay on his spider map. 'It's the village of Kezabian.'

'Or at least it was,' said the young American. 'It looks like it's been hit by a twister.'

'Tornadoes don't leave tyre tracks.' Jackson was looking at several deep V-shaped markings that criss-crossed a path to the river's edge.

'Time we gathered some evidence,' he said, turning his dot.robot towards the flattened carcass of an unrecognizable wooden structure. 'Twins, take stills. Brooke and I will shoot video.'

Jackson swept low over the site, framing the cinderblock scars of two complete rows of houses that formed perfect rectangles in the sludge. Then something caught his attention, something pristine among the chaos.

It was hard to make out exactly what the polished steel object was until, with a few nimble nudges, the Kojima twins pushed back the branches and plastic sheeting that concealed it.

'It's a valve,' said Brooke, hovering her remobot above the dinner-plate-sized metal wheel of a huge tap, screwed into a concrete slab in the ground. 'And I'm guessin' it leads straight from the river,' she added.

As they skulked along the hedgerows and thickets that lined the route from the vanished village to their final destination just a few kilometres north-west, the telltale tyre tracks ominously pointed the way. Whatever vehicles had made the markings, they had evidently torn a straight line across flat scrubland and meadows, leaving thick clots of mud on the roads that even the morning's rainstorm had failed to wash away. *We're hot on the heels of whoever made these*, Jackson told himself.

'This is it, the end of the line,' he said, as the foursome perched their MeX$_1$s on a grassy ridge. Even the swirling rain couldn't hide what lay beyond them, the jagged contour of the Carpathian mountain range, black against the clouds. A gaping hole had been cut from the base of the biggest mountain. In front of the newly quarried cave was a pound filled with trucks – big rigs, many of them with three huge box trailers linked up behind.

'Strange place for a truck fest,' said Jackson.

'Sure is, and I'm guessin' the folks behind the barriers ain't spectators.' Brooke was referring to an angry mob, separated from the compound by a ring of chain-link fence and what looked like armed guards.

'We need to get closer to record all this,' said Jackson. 'Brooke, d'you think you can fly down there and get a close-up on those trucks?'

'I'll get closer than a bumper sticker!' said the American.

'We do . . . people,' added Miss Kojima.

'Great. I'll keep a check of things from up here. And remember what Lear said, guys – use your eyes and ears but keep a lid on it – no one must know we're here. Just gather your evidence and meet back up here.'

'I'll be a regular Kojak with a Kodak,' said Brooke as the three grey discs, controlled by her and the twins, slunk over the cliff's edge and blended into the under-belly of the storm.

Miss Kojima's machine was sitting just a few metres from a fat man with a very big machine gun. He should have been keeping lookout, but he was more interested in devouring a family-sized box of doughnuts, chomping on a stack of three at a time, while listening to his jeep's radio. He was still a problem, though, one that she and her brother needed to solve if they were to pass un-detected through the gateway he was guarding. The twins had dropped into the compound easily enough from the steep escarpment that formed part of the perimeter, but to have a good view of the crowd they needed to get out the other side.

'I need your assistance, brother,' she said in Japanese. They had risen to the giddy heights of Japan's professional gaming leagues by honing a repertoire of special moves, a secret repertoire inspired by a miscellany of their ancient country's most revered comic-book characters and ninja fighting movies, of which they had amassed formidable collections.

'I am ready, sister,' the nine-year-old replied.

'Samurai Spook,' said his sister softly. The subtle cue was all the boy gamer needed to slide his MeX_1 out from behind a pile of sand and steal his way round the rotund security guard.

Brooke was looking at a reflection of her MeX_1 in the polished metal grille of a massive Mack truck on the edge of a vehicle park, its long chain of three trailers stretching the full length of the compound.

'I'm thinking sixteen axles . . . about fifty-five metres long . . . she'll carry a little over a hundred tonnes.'

'Brooke, I hope you're filming. We haven't come all this way so you can pick up facts for your scrapbook,' said Jackson.

'She's a road-train. The biggest momma on the highway. They're used to haul heavy freight around the yellow-belly states. And there are what . . . ten of them in this yard? That's still only a thousand tonnes. I'm just saying, that ain't a lot of water.'

Jackson realized she was right; you couldn't drain a river like the one they'd just seen even if you filled a thousand trailers.

'I've got an idea,' announced Brooke. 'Am I clear to move in?'

Moving deeper inside the vehicle park would mean Brooke playing cat and mouse with a couple of overalled workers and mean-looking security men. From his perch, Jackson could see both guards were heavily tooled-up; dual shoulder holsters trimmed with ammunition magazines were strapped tightly over army-green jumpsuits, and each carried a large automatic weapon. He couldn't be sure at this distance, but he assumed they'd be connected to some kind of radio network and if Brooke's bot was spotted, the game would be up for the whole team.

'I'm not sure we can risk it,' said Jackson tentatively. But it was too late. Brooke's MeX$_1$ was gliding slowly down a narrow passage created by the hulks of six heavy haulers.

'Brooke! Well, if you insist, there's a mechanic at your three o'clock and he's coming straight for you!'

'Fool with a tool, I see him,' she replied, catching sight of the workman's boots through the six sets of hefty wheels that held up the truck cabin. Brooke swung her dot.robot hard left. Jackson watched as her grey disc nipped beneath the shiny battery box that hung below the cabin door like a big chrome coffin, a milli-second before an unsuspecting mechanic appeared from round the front of the vehicle.

'I am ready, sister,' said Master Kojima.

'Good, then let loose the spirit.'

The boy's MeX$_1$ darted behind a grouping of tin shacks, carefully scraping the side of his machine against their corrugated metal walls and making the noise you get when you run a stick along railings.

The sentry, who was using a penknife to coax the final morsels from a jar of something, looked up and then began to walk the twenty or so paces to the line of makeshift toilets behind which the silver saucer hid.

Samurai Spook referred to one of an assortment of secret strategies that the guileful gaming duo could rely on. Double Trouble, Soul Diva, Kewojema Kiss, Demon's Tooth, all cryptic names that within the quick-fire world of the first-person shooter might involve faking an empty that would draw an opportunistic opponent out and into the path of your teammate's head-shot or, in the brinkmanship of a real-time strategy tournament, the construction of a phony base which would lead to your enemy squandering valuable resources in attacking it. Feints and ruses, used by two players at the top of their game. And the cryptic language was necessary as, in the world of competition gaming, there were spies everywhere – crafty snoopers who would blend in with the other spectators, eavesdrop on conversations and share their findings with the other teams by means of a series of coded hand gestures. This kind of espionage existed wherever there was money to be made, and that was certainly the case in the hallowed halls that hosted the big-money E-Sports tournaments, where a $500,000 prize could be the result of a successfully concealed unit or an unexpected special move.

The guard stood before the line of tin-shack toilets, probing his teeth with a splinter, wondering if it was another one of those infernal wild dogs who, bewitched by the smell of the slop, lifted up the flap at the back of the outhouse and got trapped inside. He wasn't sure which was worse, having to get out of his bunk at 3 a.m. to put a stop to their wretched howling, or the quiet ones who waited for you to take a seat then started growling and snapping at your *gluteus maximus*. He gingerly opened the first door and peered inside. Nothing more than noxious fumes. *Why is it*, he thought, *that these slops are cleaned out every day, but it always smells like someone has curled up and died in here?* Suddenly something hit the door behind the guard, pushing him inside the fetid room, and forcing him to inhale its vicious stench again. Then the next door banged and the one after that, until all six doors had been slammed against their rickety frames. Jumping back out into the rain with a vigour befitting a much thinner man, the two-metre ogre brought up both fists and proceeded to open each door in turn.

'If that's you, Jameson,' he shouted angrily, 'you'd best be ready to take your licks this time!'

When he had reached the end of the line, the guard was thoroughly confused, not to mention fuming. It certainly wasn't the dogs. *And that jug-head Jameson isn't anywhere to be seen*, he thought, glancing round the back of the huts. Then he saw the door slowly opening, at the far end of the line. He still couldn't see anyone, but he was sure by the way it had opened and shut that someone had just gone inside.

'If this is your idea of fun, then fine!' the guard shouted. 'I'm off back to my post.' Except he wasn't. He crept along the front of the cabins like a lion with a scent, towards the end door. *Just one more door*, thought the portly guard. *And I'll wipe the smile off his smug little face.*

He managed to sneak past five doors without making a sound, hanging his big square head below the gap under each. The guard had lost count of how many times he'd been the butt of one of Jameson's pranks. There was the time he'd had Tabasco and red-hot wasabi sauce poured into his water canteen. His boots had been filled with peanut butter. And on the one day he'd been tasked with taking the boss to the airport, he'd found his jeep jacked-up on bricks. Revenge would be sweet. Brutal and sweet.

There was no longer any need for Master Kojima to keep his machine in the vicinity of the toilet block as his sister was long gone. But haunting the gullible guard was just too enjoyable and ever since Brooke had used the HAIL function during their Cambodian temple mission, he'd been itching to give it a try.

With his saucer wedged between the slops bucket and the access flap at the back of the shack, he waited patiently until the enraged sentry swung the toilet door open.

'Gotcha!' the fat man bellowed as he rushed inside, only to find the cubicle vacant.

With his dot.robot's searchlight glowing from the foul depths of the wooden hole, over which the guard squatted at least twice a day, Master Kojima started to speak, in his most enigmatic Japanese. The mysterious chanting drifted up through the hole and echoed around the shack's metal walls. What for the guard had started out as yet more of his workmate's shenanigans had turned into something genuinely unnerving.

Pull yourself together, man, he told himself. *That snivelling little mickey-taker has got to be somewhere*. And with that, he lurched forward and pulled up the hinged plank that formed the toilet seat. To his utter amazement, the bright beam of a searchlight flashed in his face – and as his vision cleared, he saw the edge of what looked like a miniature flying saucer slipping under the flap.

The portly guard left the line of toilets faster than he ever thought his overweight legs would carry him.

Even with the guard running away, questioning his sanity after the actions of her brother's machine, the risk of being spotted was too great to take her MeX$_1$ over the fence, so Miss Kojima sent her machine low over the wet ground, slipping it silently below the unattended barrier. Boxing around the compound, the cunning girl gamer positioned her flying machine a safe distance from the edge of the crowd. Men, women and several small children stood side by side, waving their fists in the air. One woman carried a small child in a basket on her back and a tiny baby slung across her front. And there were old folks, beating their walking sticks on the fence and shouting at the expressionless men in green on the other side.

'Jackson, you must see,' Miss Kojima called over the intercom, as she sent her surveillance shots into the bottom left of Jackson's screen. The threadbare bunch must have been refugees from the vanished village. They must have stood up to Dragos . . . refused to bow down to his demands. But however passionate their protest, it was small comfort for them now, with their homes lying shattered in the muddy remains of their once proud river.

That's why we've been sent here, Jackson thought reso-
lutely. *We are here so that MeX can show what this thieving
dog is doing.* But where *was* their water?

Then Brooke revealed it all.

CHAPTER 18

'Run that by me again,' said Jackson.

'Like I said,' said the American, 'it's in the rock. This mountain is one big ol' reservoir! From the outside these rigs look like grand old freight shakers. But the trailers are stuffed full of coiled-up pipe. You gettin' my video feed all right?'

Jackson was indeed receiving a smooth feed from Brooke's camera as her remobot peered through a gap in the doors of one of the trailers. Inside were several rows of what looked like giant cotton reels with thick flattened hosing, almost half a metre wide, wound tightly round each.

'The eighteen-wheelers are the pumps – these fifty-wheelers are the pipes!'

Brooke reversed her MeX$_1$ and swung round to reveal the full extent of the man-made cavity hewn from the mountain. It formed a large cave, twice as tall as the biggest truck and wide enough to fit four abreast.

'There's a pipe exchange at the base of the mountain.

One end of a convoy pulls up and plugs in. I'm guessin' it wouldn't take long for a daisy chain of triples to turn a creek as dry as a redneck's bath towel. Judgin' by the fresh car-boogers on these wheel arches, I'd say these is the rigs we were chasin'.'

But before a stunned Jackson could ask any more questions, Miss Kojima's voice cut in on the intercom. 'Excuse me. We have company. Four jeeps . . . from north.'

Jackson tracked them from his clifftop position. A convoy of vehicles bounced and splashed their way towards camp. As the vehicles rounded the narrow entrance to the ravine, he could see there were actually three 4x4s and a pick-up truck with six men in the back. They were wearing normal clothes, rather than the pea-green khaki of their friends in the camp, but they were sturdy men with thick necks and broad shoulders, and Jackson was sure they were more of Dragos's men. *They've probably been out on reconnaissance*, he thought, *scouting for more places to plunder . . . dressed in civvies, so they blend in.* As they pulled up, a handful of guards came out to greet them.

'We need the faces of these people,' Jackson said quickly. 'Miss Kojima, are you getting this?'

'*Un.*'

As the new arrivals climbed from their vehicles, Jackson instantly recognized the raven hair of one man.

Even with most of his face obscured beneath a beret and high-collared overcoat, it was clearly the infamous General Dragos himself. And Miss Kojima was getting it all on camera, snapshot after snapshot of crystal-clear close-ups. It was perfect. They had the demolished village, the poor victims and – thanks to their intrepid American engineer – a thorough account of how the whole operation worked. But, most satisfying of all, Dragos himself at the scene of the crime. Every frame, safely stored in real-time on a MeX server. He didn't know it yet, but this was one megalomaniac whose number was up.

None of Jackson's team was close enough to hear anything, but they could see Dragos was angry. He stood outside the guardhouse, rain dripping down his face, flailing his arms about and shouting at the guards. Several times he motioned aggressively towards the crowd, stabbing his finger in their direction and then back at the group of security men. And the fuming figure of the dark-haired oil baron turned water thief lost nothing of its animation as he was ushered inside the building.

'He's not happy with the demonstration,' said Jackson. *Good*, he thought. *I hope they get right under your skin, you greedy worm.*

Then the sound of gunfire ricocheted through the valley, and all hell broke loose.

*

For a moment Jackson was too surprised to do anything. People were running everywhere: guards, men, women and children. A wave of protesters surged back from the fence, some of the less athletic falling to the ground, pressed into the mud by the desperate stampede. The guards were crouched behind vehicles and walls, letting off volley after volley of shots in the direction of the crowd. Jackson watched as one enraged protester ran at the fence, climbing its chain links in seconds and leaping at a guard on the other side. It looked for a moment as if he might win the struggle for the other man's rifle, until two more men in green joined the fight, beating him mercilessly with their rifle butts. Jackson thought he saw a scarlet mist burst from the man before his stout body went limp.

'The guards are firing on the crowd! We've got to help them!' Jackson yelled, and without thinking sent his machine over the lip of the cliff and down towards the compound.

Brooke, who had brought her remobot to the entrance of the vehicle park, had her video camera focused on a group of guards. The three heavily armed men were leaning out from behind a large yellow digger, taking pot shots.

'I'm assuming you're getting my feed, Jackson,' said Brooke. 'Permission to take them down.'

'Do it!' he instantly replied.

Brooke threw her MeX_1 towards the men, dipping its leading edge so the powerful lift fan could propel it to maximum speed. As one of the guards stepped out from behind the digger's bonnet, his rifle raised for another shot, Brooke's machine collided with him from behind. The man was thrown forward like a ragdoll, headbutting the digger's metal bonnet, knocked out cold.

'Attaboy! You just lie down and shut up!' she said, sweeping her saucer high up through the air and turning round for another pass.

The remaining two guards were quick to react, shielding themselves behind the chunky vehicle, spraying automatic gunfire towards her remobot. But Brooke had the advantage, her machine screaming down from above them, their shots wildly off course due to the driving rainfall that stung their eyes.

Time for the Kryptonite, Brooke thought, and brought up the BASS BOMB menu. She was a moment from launching the gut-busting acoustic device when her MeX_1 was hit by a barrage of heavy rounds from the opposite direction. It was like a huge hammer had swung down from the heavens and swatted her machine out of the sky. One minute she had the frantic guards in her sights, the next her screen was pitch black.

'Well, I'll be darned . . . I done got shot!' she said, flabbergasted.

*

Master Kojima pushed his bot to its limit as he hunted the unfortunate guard he had already spooked to within an inch of his life. He might have been content to let the unfortunate man run away, but since the firing had started he feared the guard might be on his way to pick up his rifle and join in. He found him at the wheel of his jeep, winding through the camp at high speed. The young Japanese boy's prowess with his futuristic flying machine was impressive. Throwing it on to its side, he pushed it through the open door of the barracks, performing a perfect knife-edge manoeuvre through the building and straight out the other end. Now in front of the jeep, he brought his MeX_1 to an instant halt. In turn, the guard slammed his brakes on until the two machines were facing each other, motionless in the rain.

The man at the wheel of the 4x4 was shaking so much he could hardly get the rusty vehicle into reverse, his sweaty palms slipping on the polished plastic of the steering wheel as he tried to find full lock. The instant the leather gear knob told him he'd found the slot, he slammed the accelerator pedal to the floor and man and vehicle swung violently backwards. It might not have looked like it, but the frantically fleeing man knew how to handle his vehicle. Before this job, he had spent ten years as a bodyguard, and the 'reverse slide 180' was standard escape-and-pursuit stuff when you had a VIP onboard. Today *he* was the VIP he was trying to protect and the second he sensed the wheels starting to drift freely, he knew it was time to find first gear and get out of there. But in a flash of blinding light his vehicle died. The engine stopped roaring and the tension went from the steering wheel. Worse still, he couldn't even see. His eyes were burning.

Master Kojima had timed the release of his Dazzler to perfection, frying the car's electrics as it careered backwards with maximum revs, leaving the useless metal husk to roll down a rocky incline, the face of its driver glassy-eyed with terror.

From his saucer's position, circling high over the compound, Jackson noticed the jeep freewheeling backwards at considerable speed. He watched as it ploughed through the canteen tent, dragging the entire structure with it before turning over in the garbage pit. But he missed the irony of the blinded driver who loved his food so much crawling out into a sea of rotting potato peelings and putrid leftovers.

Jackson switched his attention to the building that housed Dragos. *You don't even have the courage to do your own dirty work,* he thought, *hiding away like a coward!* He instructed the twins to send their machines to meet his at the entrance to the valley. But before he could rendezvous with the Kojimas, he spotted a small group of armed guards advancing towards several defenceless protesters huddled in a ditch at the roadside.

He dived his MeX_1 towards the gleaming asphalt of the road that led out of the compound, pulling up behind the thin green line of armed men as he released his Bass Bomb. The four men and their two guard dogs fell like flies. Jackson couldn't see their faces, he was already too high above, but the sight of their bodies writhing in the mud told him his Bass Bomb had hit its target.

The three remaining remobots formed up on the road, several hundred metres from the barrier that marked the entrance to the compound. The storm had reached maturity and driven by heaving winds, the rain drilled into the dot.robots' plastic shells with deafening effect. Even at full zoom, the deluge made it hard for Jackson to make out exactly how many armed men were positioning themselves along the front of the compound's buildings.

'There must be a couple of shooters hidden in the hills or something like that,' said Brooke. The American's MeX_1 was down, but she was still able to patch into her teammates' video feeds. 'I'm sure I saw a flash or two. Keep it low and quick and you should be OK.'

As they started their run, Jackson wasn't even sure what the three of them would do when they reached the camp. But they were determined Dragos should know they were going to get him somehow.

The incoming fire was intense. A couple of times Jackson felt his MeX_1 get knocked off course as a bullet found its way through the robot's soft polypropylene fuselage and embedded itself in the Kevlar casing that shielded all its vital components. Without saying a word, the brother-and-sister duo closed their vehicles together, forming a protective barrier between Jackson's machine and the incoming fire, the first of the twins' saucers a metre or so above the ground and the second piggy-backing a few millimetres above it, just as they had done at their first training exercise. Jackson watched as the two grey discs in front of his took round after round of small-arms fire until chunks of their outer casing bounced off his camera lens. Suddenly both of the Kojimas' machines exploded in quick succession, bursting into flames and hitting the floor.

'I down!' shouted Master Kojima.

'Me also,' his sister added calmly.

'It's those snipers . . . it's got to be,' said Brooke, who was looking at the smouldering wreckage of Master Kojima's MeX_1 through the flickering and juddering video feed of his sister's downed machine.

Jackson pressed on. There was nothing else for it. At least, he thought, his remobot was drawing fire away from the people who were still fleeing. There was a slim chance he could ram or even use the Dazzler against Dragos. But, just metres away from the open door of the main building, Jackson felt the control of his MeX$_1$ start to ebb away. He struggled to keep it flying, but it was hit and there was nothing he could do to stop its erratic corkscrew descent towards the ground. Jackson winced as his machine smacked into the side of a car.

Before his dot.robot's video feed went black, Jackson saw the face of the monstrous mastermind behind all this. Rain dripped off General Dragos's black beret as he walked out from the guardroom and into the rain to stand over Jackson's machine. There was a strange look of bewilderment on his raw-boned face before it was blocked out by the blinding flashes of machine-gun fire as the guards closed in.

CHAPTER 19

Devlin Lear's body language was all wrong. He kept standing up so the four of them could only see the bright yellow tartan material that covered his stomach and his gold belt buckle. And he was pacing around so much that for long periods of time he disappeared from view completely.

'Could you sit down please, Devlin?' said Brooke. 'I find video works best when there's something other than a pot belly to look at.'

Jackson flinched at the stony look on Lear's face. He and the Kojimas remained sensibly silent.

'We've already told you,' Brooke continued. 'We didn't just punk out . . . we were under attack!'

'Yes, from the guards' machine-gun fire, which you have been well trained to avoid!' Lear angrily retorted as he sat back down.

'No!' said Brooke and Jackson simultaneously.

'They couldn't see us most of the time,' Brooke protested. 'There had to be someone else out there.'

'Yes, like you said, Miss English . . . *shooters* . . . in the hills.'

'No! Look, I know I said that at the time, but you should have seen the way we went down. It was like *Boom*! Like we were hit by something explosive. We just blew up. This wasn't the work of a sniper rifle – it was as if someone had a tank up there . . . an invisible one.'

'That's enough, Miss English!' Lear exclaimed, obviously frustrated. He settled himself, tugging down his bright yellow plaid waistcoat before speaking more calmly. 'I have reviewed the footage from your mission and it is clear that Dragos's militiamen attacked the crowd and then attacked you when you unwisely came to their aid; contrary, I may say, to your orders, which were simply to observe.'

Jackson looked at the floor. Lear was right. They had disobeyed orders and revealed themselves to the enemy. But what they'd done had been the *right* thing to do. Hadn't it?

Lear seemed to sense Jackson's regret and looked at him with a degree of sympathy through the video feed. 'This . . . calamity is yet another example of the flagrant ineptitude of the international community, who are happy for us to mop up their spills, but leave us defenceless in the face of attack. Suffice it to say, a report has been filed which makes mention of small-arms fire and the *possibility* of snipers. But I can assure you it does not include anything about *invisible tanks.*'

'Enough already with the snipers!' said Brooke who was now red in the face. 'We were moving way too fast for that . . . I'm telling you, it was some big ol' heat seeker or something.'

'Miss English! That will be all on the matter!' barked Lear.

'We got Dragos bang to rights, didn't we?' asked Jackson, desperate to prove to their mentor that what they'd done had been worth something to MeX. And before his American Rottweiler of a teammate said something they might all regret. 'Isn't that what really matters? There must be enough material to show to the authorities?'

'Authorities?' Lear sighed. 'What authorities?'

'The police? I dunno.' Jackson was beginning to feel the familiar pangs of foolishness that certain people brought out in him and it felt wrong coming from Lear. 'We got enough on him to lock him away for good, didn't we?'

'Your faith in truth and justice, Farley, is noble. But wildly misguided. The footage you and your team gathered will be extremely useful in establishing Dragos's guilt. But you'd do well to understand that certain men are beyond the law.'

'Excuse me, sir.' Miss Kojima's quiet voice, which

hadn't been heard once during the whole exchange, was enough to stop everyone speaking. 'When . . . will be . . . next mission?'

Jackson felt his stomach drop. It was the question he had most wanted to ask but had been too afraid of Lear's response. Despite all of Brooke's protesting and his attempt at justifying their actions, Jackson felt responsible for the mission's failure. He'd followed Lear's plan to the letter and, even now, as they sifted through the wreckage of the Ukrainian assignment, he couldn't explain why it had gone so wrong.

'It might be an idea to let all this blow over for a while. I will be in touch.' And with that, Lear was gone.

Jackson yawned. He had spent hours in front of his computer. He hadn't even dressed or cleaned his teeth, just rolled straight out of bed and plugged in.

With no contact from Lear or the others on his MeX handset, Jackson had checked his email in desperation for some sign that their mistakes had been resolved and he would be needed to lead another exciting mission. But the only mails that caught his attention were one from his dad's work address, reminding him to buy the sunflowers for his mum's grave, and a message from Mr Willard about Monday's chess club, entitled *Chess, the Game of Kings*. And then, to distract himself from the sick feeling that he'd mucked up everything, he logged into *Whisper* and checked WizardZombie was where he'd left him, asleep next to the burnt-out embers of his fire: health 70%.

It didn't work. Jackson needed some air. He threw on some clothes and headed down into the quadrangle at the base of his block of flats.

The events of the last twenty-four hours were taking their toll. Jackson couldn't sleep – he couldn't get the faces of those refugees out of his head. Where were they now? Had Dragos's men hurt any more of them? He'd hoped Lear's request to convene a group meeting would make sense of the whole thing, but it was clear that he and the other recruits weren't being offered their usual access to MeX information after their botched attempt to intervene. He hoped desperately that this wasn't a permanent MeX measure.

It was already impressively hot outside, even in the long shadows thrown by the towerblocks. Having left the flat in the hope that some fresh air might help straighten out the muddle in his head, Jackson soon found himself wandering away from the relative calm of the estate and towards the familiar hubbub of the high street. It was as if some internal sat-nav was guiding him towards a plan of action, because before long he had turned down the side street that led to his local Internet cafe – The Zap Shack.

The cafe had a dedicated gaming section in the basement. Jackson had spent more after-school hours here than he knew were good for him, surfacing only for pizza and once or twice to an embarrassing confrontation with his dad, wanting to know why he wasn't home yet. As soon as Jackson reached the cafe's neon-blue opening, and saw the banks of computers inside, he hit on an idea. If he could find something that would incriminate Dragos beyond all doubt, then perhaps Lear would welcome them back to finish the job they had started.

Jackson bought a Coke and a sandwich containing something masquerading as chicken. He decided to opt for a terminal upstairs today, because he couldn't stomach the idea of consuming food in the clammy downstairs dungeon – its atmosphere fermented by the bodily functions of thirty teenagers who, given it was Sunday morning, had probably stayed the night in there.

Upstairs the cafe was bright and airy, with concertina doors that opened out on to an alley. It wasn't exactly pretty, but if you had the right seat you could see the sky while you surfed and feel the wind on your face, which was a welcome relief from the umpteen kilowatts of heat produced by a roomful of computers. As Jackson waited for a page to load, he could see that the bright, warm morning was turning fickle. *Rain now*, he thought, *but be bright for tomorrow. Be bright for Mum.*

Tomorrow would mark the third anniversary of his

mother's death and Jackson and his dad were going to visit her grave. His dad was working nights and Jackson had special permission to leave school early. They were both under strict instructions to be 'happy'. 'Do something you really enjoy!' she'd instructed them. 'Only talk about the good times . . . and bring sunflowers.' He wanted so much to do as he was told, to follow his mum's instructions to the letter, unlike last year. They'd tried really hard; his dad had even broken out a suit and a tie so loud it threatened to wake up some of the graveyard's inhabitants. But in the end they'd just stood there, crying, and being thoroughly disobedient.

Thinking about his mum also, weirdly, made him think of Brooke. He'd been unable to contact her, which was a little odd. Even the twins were unavailable, but Jackson was sure this was due to their packed schedule of professional gaming tournaments. He remembered how Brooke had been seething about the meeting with Lear – and tired as well, on account of the time difference. But Jackson hoped she wasn't mad at him for not speaking as much as she had at the meeting. He had just wanted the team's efforts to be recognized, with the satisfaction and sense of respect that brought.

Jackson finished the last crumbs of his rubbery sandwich and stared at the screen, more determined than ever to discover whatever underhanded tactics Dragos had used to bring them down. The cursor in the search box blinked like an excited heartbeat. Something about it reminded him of the blips they'd seen on their radars – blips they'd managed to explain away. But the feeling that something had been stalking them remained. Jackson left his thoughts hanging as his fingers automatically started typing: *Invisible tanks with heat-seeking missiles.*

It was as good a place to start as any.

Jackson sat back, looking at the reams of results that his search had brought up, and marvelled at the varying degrees of relevancy – *build your own tropical fish tank!* He imagined the web spiders that had crawled all over these pages, virtual insects made of pure code, burrowing into the World Wide Web, collecting, copying and indexing all its pages, at his command. Jackson started to feel a bit better – this was the world he felt comfortable in. A world he knew more about than most. It was why Lear had chosen him and he was going to use his skills to get them all out of this mess.

His attention was suddenly drawn to an entry for the Global Patent and Trademark Office. It was a domain he wasn't entirely unfamiliar with. Every new invention had to be registered and this was the place to do it. Jackson knew it was standard practice among the bloggers and forum administrators who traded in techno-rumour-mongering to trawl sites like this for evidence of new gaming devices and gadgets.

Jackson's search had landed him at patent application number #5112-11877. Real Holdings Ltd's System for Active Optical Camouflage. Notwithstanding the entry's dense legal-speak, it described a means of making a vehicle 'invisible' by using an array of video cameras and what Jackson understood to be a razor-thin flexible screen that could be wrapped like a skin round whatever you wanted to hide.

Straight out of Star Trek, Jackson thought, poring over a series of diagrams and blueprints that showed a cube covered in what amounted to a stretchy TV screen that could be rolled out and stuck on like wallpaper. As he waded through endless plans, attempting to decipher paragraph after paragraph of lawyer-speak, he slowly built up an understanding of the amazing invention. Four tiny cameras stuck on the skin covering an object or vehicle filmed everything around it. Then – just like computer games wrap textures around shapes – the cameras fed what they saw on to the special wafer-thin video skin that covered every centimetre of the object. In one artist's impression, a tank had been drawn, surrounded by a ring of clumsily etched Christmas trees, each with a unique number beside it. It was clear that from whichever angle the tank was viewed, the corresponding background of numbered fir trees was visible. But the tank was not.

He continued to skim through the document, looking for headlines:

Invention Summary

An invention is provided for concealing a vehicle.

Our Active Optical Camouflage system offers a solution for 'total invisibility' when used in conjunction with standard Infra-red and Radar evasion packages. Using a matrix of OLEDs (Organic Light Emitting Diodes) that make up our flexible Optical Skin™, it is possible to 'cloak' most of the distinguishing features of a given vehicle. An advanced graphics processor reliably predicts said vehicle's movement through even the most visually complex of environments – including forests, mountains and urban surroundings – and is able to cope with the effects of harsh sunlight and shadowing.

Brief Description of Effect

At the optimal viewing distance, defined here as +20 metres, the object is not visible to the naked eye, other than a faint shimmering effect and barely perceptible colour phasing caused by light refraction.

On an impulse Jackson returned to the top of the document, checked the company name and entered it into the domain's own search box.

Let's see if Real Holdings Ltd has invented anything else.

A list of hundreds of exotic-sounding contraptions filled the screen, organized in date order, the most recent at the top. Most meant nothing to him but, after browsing several pages, a few entries caught Jackson's eye.

- 5113-98554 Experimental liquid breathing system
- 5113-98544 Apparatus for emitting underwater pressure pulse
- 5113-98541 Flexible-plastic submersible boat hull
- 5113-98523 Memory-metal underwater propulsion system

Cool! But irrelevant . . .

He scrolled further down.

- 5112-11873 Automated target tracking system for aerial vehicle
- 5112-11861 Aluminium camera mounting for aerial vehicle
- 5112-11860 Titanium barrel for explosive projectiles

A picture was slowly starting to emerge. Jackson felt a buzz of excitement building in his stomach as he realized he was looking at everything required to build the kind of machine Brooke thought had shot the team down. There were also entries that described drilling equipment and something called 'plastic rock amalgam'. There, in black and white, was a description of the technology Dragos would need for his Ukrainian operation – and Jackson couldn't wait to tell Lear.

Then he noticed some of the company's earlier applications for patent protection.

- 5112-11521 High-power, low-weight electrical fuel cell
- 5112-11520 Method for directing and ducting airflow
- 5112-11513 Aeronautical thermoplastic with stealth characteristics

That was odd. It read like a shopping list for the components of their MeX$_1$ remobots. Jackson recalled Lear's first briefing on the MeX$_1$ ... *electrically powered, getting the juice for its ducted fan engine from fuel-cell batteries.* What was going on? Could Dragos have access to MeX technology without Lear's knowledge? Jackson imagined the MeX$_1$ with another of the company's patented inventions, 'active optical camouflage'. *An invisible flying machine with a dirty great cannon on board.*

Something didn't feel right. How had MeX technology been so easily accessed and used against them? This was so much more serious than the recruits' failed mission. Jackson knew he had to contact Lear and tell him everything he'd just found out.

He pounded home, eager to access the MeX handset that he'd unoriginally hidden under his bed, away from prying parental eyes.

In his hurry he fell out of the lift as it reached the floor to his flat.

His dad stood waiting for him, filling the empty doorway. 'I think you have some explaining to do, young man.'

CHAPTER 20

His dad was fuming. Jackson had forgotten to buy the sunflowers. He stood in the kitchen, taking everything his dad verbally threw at him. He understood why he was mad. As far as his dad could see, Jackson had got up late and been out all afternoon with his 'gaming buddies'. His dad had even sent a polite reminder by email, which was his way of saying how important the flowers were, but Jackson had still failed to deliver.

Jackson knew that this was just his dad's way of dealing with feeling so sad. It was like this every year. But he still felt awful – he knew he should have been spending more time with his dad. Jackson just needed to speak to Lear now to clear this mess up, then he would definitely find more time in between missions. It would be different from now on.

'Dad, I'm sorry. I'll sort everything out. There's still time before tomorrow. I promise,' said Jackson. Then, slipping guiltily out of the lounge, he went straight to his room.

As Jackson fumbled around for the MeX handset and the pen and coins that he had wrapped in a sports sock under his bed, the muffled refrain of 'Rule Britannia' gently rang out.

He pulled the package out and let the phone flop on to his desk, before eagerly picking it up and hitting the green ANSWER key.

'Hello. Who is this?' said the monotone woman's voice.

'It's me . . . it's Jackson Farley.'

'Voice identification positive for Jackson Farley. Initiating secure voice call.'

There was a click, followed by a brief pause, and then Lear surprised Jackson by speaking to him directly.

171

'Ah, Farley. How are you?'

'Mr Lear, I've been trying to reach you. I've found details of several inventions which –'

'Look, I'll get straight to the point,' Lear interrupted abruptly. 'I know what you've found. I think it might be a good idea if both of us put our cards on the table.'

Jackson was gobsmacked. Was Lear talking about this afternoon's surfing session in the cafe? How did he know what Jackson had been looking at?

'The Global Patent and Trademark Office,' said Lear. 'You've got to laugh really, all the effort we go to, to keep things hush-hush, but we've still got to register them in broad daylight, otherwise someone else will claim they invented them first. Of course, sometimes the best way to hide something is to put it out in the open. Still, I have to say I'm impressed by your ingenuity, Farley. I always have been. So, what do you think of the clever inventions of Real Holdings Ltd?'

'I'm not sure what you mean?' A horrible suspicion was starting to make Jackson feel uncomfortable. And he wasn't sure he wanted to hear what was coming next.

'I kept tabs on all four of you for a while, as part of my selection process. And you, Farley, you really are a special case. I expected a lot from you and yet you've managed to exceed my expectations at every stage.'

Jackson remained silent.

'Just ask yourself why the other three follow you, Farley, and you might understand that you and I are not so different. They follow you, like you follow me.'

'We're a team!' Jackson protested. 'And I don't follow you . . .' His voice trailed off. He knew that to some extent what Lear was saying was true.

'Come now, you've followed me from the start. From that first Messenger contact you let Elan Drivel take the lead. As you yourself discovered, Farley, *I* am Elan Drivel. And what is it about MeX that you believe in? Those ideals? The desire you have deep down to make something of yourself and use your unique abilities to do something positive? Those are my ideals and my desires too. Surely, someone of your intelligence can't fail to see the potential behind the technologies we're developing?'

Lear's words washed around Jackson's head. He wasn't sure about anything any more – neither his invisible gunship theory nor Lear's strange behaviour in the mission debriefing. What the businessman was saying made sense. After all, Lear had seen something in Jackson from the beginning. It was strange, but the drive and single-mindedness that had made Lear so successful – along with his commitment and dedication to developing the MeX organization – these were qualities that Jackson respected and aspired to. But at the same time there were still so many unanswered questions.

Jackson shook his head, trying to clear the confusion. There was one thing he needed to know first of all. Something he needed to hear Lear say.

'It was you, wasn't it? You're the one stealing the water. Dragos had nothing to do with it!'

Lear didn't reply immediately. Jackson could hear him draw a deep breath or even sigh, as if the effort required to answer the question made him weary. 'Dragos is a player in this game, as we are all players. His innocence or guilt, or mine, in all of this is unimportant. The fight to control the precious commodity of water in that region, just like similar fights the world over, will happen regardless of the right or wrong of it. Would you rather tens of billions of dollars of water be squandered or left at the behest of morally impoverished government officials? Don't you think that with proper management, with the kind of technology MeX has at its disposal, that we are better suited to governing something so precious?'

Jackson felt sick. He couldn't believe it had all been a big lie.

'And who is Dragos? Someone who stood up to you, I suppose? You set us up to make him look guilty, didn't you? You sent us there and used some secret invisible MeX unit to shoot us down and make it look as if Dragos had done it all.'

'It's called the Cloaker. The MeX$_3$ is my most advanced dot.robot yet. Invisible and deadly even at long range. What can I say, Farley . . . it's progress. It's going to save us all. Think about it. We are on the verge of a new and magical technological age. Who holds the keys to our future? Who will lift us into space and beyond? The sleazy politicians? The snivelling bureaucrats who squander everything? Or the innovators and businessmen, like me, who by sheer force of will are responsible for our scientific progress?'

'How is flattening a village "progress"?'

'Don't be so short-sighted, Farley. It's a means to a better end. The poor homeless peasants. The evil rich General Dragos. And the four Experimental Mechanicals dot.robots that try to intervene but are hopelessly out-gunned. What better way to prove the case for giving us the extra weapons we need to do our job? What was it the Kojima twins said at the end of your first MeX$_1$ test flight? *Two birds, one stone.* The governments give us the arms our robots need to help with their global security commitments, and I have them to hand when I need to secure the business deals that everyone will eventually benefit from.

'This opportunity is bigger than either of us, Farley. And if a few ragged villagers have to suffer a little incon-venience along the way, then so be it. Water is the new oil. If we are not there to soak up this opportunity, some other ineffective organization or government will be. And do you think they will care if the people of some poorer country like Ghana, Nigeria or Somalia die of thirst in the meantime?'

'Wait a minute.' Jackson's mind cut back to the first few MeX missions he and his team had undertaken. 'You said Somalia. You had us guarding food aid there last week. But that wasn't food in those shipping containers, was it? It was more of your water-pumping equipment, right? You mention those places because you're already there. You're already in those countries, stealing their water!'

'Are you really so naive?' said Lear, becoming increas-ingly agitated. 'Already, one person in five doesn't have access to safe drinking water. If we can control these markets, we can ensure that if they want it, they can have it – from us. Business first, Farley, then humanity.'

'As long as they are prepared to pay whatever price you put on it,' Jackson replied.

Lear was silent for a moment; the only sound, the static of the phone connection. Then he released a typically overdramatic sigh.

'So now you know everything, what *do* you intend to do?'

Jackson seethed with hatred for the man who had conned them all. What could he do? He couldn't exactly go to the police. *Excuse me, officer. I'm a member of a top-secret organization that uses a fleet of robotic flying saucers to fight baddies. Except the baddies have turned out to be goodies, and the goodies . . . Oh, forget it!* Jackson thought about Lear's power and fortune and realized that he was probably one of those men beyond the law, that he had not so long ago accused the innocent Dragos of being.

'If it's all the same,' said Jackson, 'I think I'll let others decide if this is just . . . business.' He was trying to sound confident, but Jackson was spooked and he wasn't sure if he was doing a very good job of covering it up.

'How is your Latin, Farley? *Testis unos, testis nullus.*

It's one of the founding principles in law. One witness is not a witness.'

'Yes, well, I'm not the only one who knows about you . . .' The words were out before he'd realized what he was saying. From the moment Jackson had realized Lear was the unprincipled and unscrupulous money-grabber he clearly was, he'd been wary of what he might be capable of. Now he had implicated his friends.

'Oh, I don't think we need worry about them; everyone has been dealt with in the way they deserve. How is Brooke by the way, Farley? I know the two of you, in particular, are close.'

It sounded like a casual remark, but it chilled Jackson to the bone. He sank into his chair, a mixture of loathing and fear radiating from his side of the phone.

'If you've done anything to Brooke or the twins –' he began.

'Now, now, Farley, there's no need to get overexcited. Let's keep things reasonable, shall we? You show me you can keep things to yourself and I'll make sure nothing happens to our mutual friends. Do we understand each other?'

Jackson was quiet. In the space of just one phone call, events had taken an abominable turn for the worse and he didn't know what to say.

'I . . . understand,' he muttered.

'Good,' said Lear, suddenly switching to a more upbeat

tone. 'I know how all this must seem to you, but I'm confident you'll soon see the bigger picture. There's more that unites you and I than divides us, you know.'

'Get lost!' Jackson spat the words into phone.

'Why don't you hang on to your MeX gear for the time being,' said Lear calmly. 'I'm afraid you won't be able to login, but that will change when you come round to my way of thinking.' And with that, he was gone.

Jackson remained frozen in his chair. He needed to make contact with Brooke and the twins, to warn them, but he was afraid there wasn't enough time.

CHAPTER 21

Jackson had been up until the early hours trying to contact Brooke. He'd emailed her over and over again with no response, and he'd looked at his Messenger window so many times her greyed-out icon was seared into the backs of his eyeballs. He tried International Directory Enquiries, where a man who sounded like he'd just walked off the set of *Night of the Living Dead* told him, 'America is a big place. I need something more specific than "the state of California".' In a last desperate attempt, Jackson had ended up dialling the number from the website for the Massachusetts Institute of Technology. What his dad would think when the twenty-minute call to the United States came up on the phone bill was next month's problem. But his one glimmer of hope was promptly extinguished.

'Can I help?' asked the assistant for J.P. English, Brooke's dad.

'I'm trying to get hold of J.P. English, or even better, Brooke. I'm a friend of hers from England.'

'I'm afraid Brooke has gone missing. J.P. is flying back home. I've come in to collect a few of his things. I'm sorry, who is this?'

Jackson hung up. He felt numb. Lear had already betrayed his slimy assurance. He had taken Brooke. Jackson hadn't received any replies to the emails he'd sent to the Kojimas either – Lear had them all. Jackson was going to do something. He would get them back. He cared about his friends – a sentiment he knew Lear wouldn't understand. And when everything looked as though it couldn't be any worse, Jackson felt slightly better – he was nothing like Lear. The smug billionaire was wrong about him. He would work at finding Brooke first because she was on her own and at least the twins had each other. He just needed to work out how to do it. He couldn't call the police; he couldn't do anything out of the ordinary for fear it might alert Lear. With his connection to MeXnet cut off he was just an ordinary Joe, trying to find three missing people who lived at opposite ends of the globe. Jackson tried to focus and shrug off the feeling that he might be being watched right now too. Was he next? He'd just have to go to school and act normally. He could continue his search for clues online, in the relative safety of school.

Jackson dressed quickly and threw a few things into his bag when he noticed the MeX handset on his bedside cabinet. The coins and pen were sitting beside it. He certainly couldn't leave them there for his dad to find. He scooped them up and dropped them into the pouch on the front of his backpack, then slid his own mobile in beside them and nervously headed out.

There was a flower stall near the bus stop. Jackson bought a bunch of about eight sunflowers, big enough to keep his dad happy, but small enough to mount vertically in his backpack since the sentiment behind them would be lost on his peers at school.

Jackson's wait for the bus was excruciating. He was convinced he was going to be grabbed at any second. Everyone was suspect. Who was the man in the black raincoat walking down the street towards him? Was he staring at him? The gang of older kids hanging out on the opposite side of the street looked incredibly shifty. He'd never seen them before. And what about the woman standing with a pram near the corner shop? Jackson couldn't hear a baby crying. Perhaps there was no baby in there at all?

Calm down, he told himself. The school bus pulled up and Jackson scrambled on it.

He dug out his mobile phone and started its minia-ture web browser. He had always found that busying himself with something 'technical' was a good way of calming his nerves. He thumbed the buttons, filling the teensy white web address field with the first address that came to mind. It took a couple of minutes for his *math-fu.com* home page to load, which wasn't too bad considering how deathly slow the Internet could be on his mobile. Checking his site for comments was part of Jackson's daily routine, but the events of the last few days had left his routine in tatters. As the 'comments' section loaded, he could see there was a message waiting for his approval, and strangely it took the shape of a short, two-line poem. For the most part visitors to his site left behind maths problems and general number trivia, the odd chess puzzler and, of course, the abusive comments that were always anonymous and always bore Hughes's hallmark. But this message was distinctive, not just because it was written in verse, but because of the name beside it. *GeekSugar.* Jackson recognized it immediately. It was Brooke's username, the one she'd sent him when she'd let him rev her Hummer.

> *Now in here least evermore I languish*
> *A brilliance of strategy is required hastily*

Jackson sat in geography, his last lesson of the day, staring at the poem scrawled inside the sweet wrapper. Two lines. Seven words in each. Whatever it was, it had managed to flummox him all day. It was a pattern, of sorts, but more than that he just didn't know.

He sighed in frustration. He was running out of time, and later this afternoon he'd be at his mum's grave . . . Jackson froze – that was it! His mum was the key. His mind shot back to his first real chat with Brooke, when she'd been fascinated by his mum's Pi poem. *She's using the Pi poem code.*

Jackson dipped a hand into his bag and retrieved a felt-tip pen. A quick glance up revealed that Mr Christy, the geography teacher, hadn't noticed what he was up to.

Mr Christy didn't have Mr Willard's natural flair for teaching, but at least he made an effort. This afternoon's lesson, on the wonders of Brazil, saw him dressed in a Brazilian football shirt. Bearing in mind that Crusty Christy was only a few years shy of a pension, it was quite impressive. He had also rearranged the desks so that they formed one large surface, on to which he'd unfolded a huge map of South America, about half of which was dominated by the continent's largest nation. At various positions on the chart, Crusty had placed objects. There were some foreign coins over Brasilia, the country's capital city, a small pile of coffee beans, a toy petrol pump in the sea near Rio de Janeiro, various plastic animals and a toy lorry with some twigs taped to its back. The students had to pick an object and talk about its relevance to Brazil. Of course, no one volunteered.

'Sarah Jacobs, I volunteer you. Which of my Brazilian knick-knacks do you feel you could tell me about?'

As Sarah leaned confidently across the map, picked up the toy lorry and proceeded to tell the class all about the destruction of the Amazonian rainforest, Jackson turned his attention to the task, quite literally, in hand.

First word? 'Now'.

Number of characters? Three.

He wrote a '3' on his left palm, the red ink from his pen filling the tiny furrows and trenches in his skin so that the number looked like it was exploding. The next word was made up of two characters, the third – four; Jackson deciphered each line until he had two rows of seven numbers, vying for space on the inside of his hand.

3   2   4   5   8   1   8
1   10   2   8   2   8   7

He stared at his open palm. It looked as if the figures were written in blood. And in a way they were, because he knew the fate of his friend was locked inside them.

Why would Brooke send me numbers? What would she expect me to do with them? He added up each line: 31 and 38. The totals meant nothing to him. He tried combining the two lines and rearranged them in size order: 1, 1, 2, 2, 2, 3, 4, 5, 7, 8, 8, 8, 8, 10. But other than the six prime numbers that Jackson was naturally drawn towards again, he saw nothing. *Don't get sidetracked*, he thought, noting his tendency to overcomplicate things as soon as numbers were around. *Brooke's an engineer, not a mathematician.*

The number ten intrigued him, though. The base of the numerical system. One more than nine. One less than his favourite number, eleven. The sum of the first three prime numbers, 2, 3 and 5. *Keep it simple*, he reminded himself. *Why a ten, why not a one and a zero? Because you can't make a word out of zero? Was that the reason?*

Jackson could feel himself getting frustrated. There was so much at stake here. He needed to focus. Instinct told him he was looking at two sets of numbers. If he accepted that the ten was nothing more significant than a means of completing the poem with a ten-letter word, then he had 3245818 and 11028287.

He sighed and looked up to see Rich Jenkins had jumped to his feet, and was trying to tackle Crusty in order to illustrate the Brazilians' love of football.

'Very good, everyone,' said Crusty, eventually gathering his breath. 'Time for a little treasure-hunting, I think.'

He started writing on the whiteboard. 'I hope you

all remember the map reading we covered last term? There are some points of interest that I've hidden in Brazil. I'd like you to find them and write a sentence on each from your textbooks.'

There was a groan from the class. When he'd finished writing, Crusty moved away from the whiteboard to reveal three sets of handwritten numbers.

$$23° \ 33' \ S \qquad 46° \ 38' \ W$$
$$30° \ 20' \ S \qquad 51° \ 13' \ W$$
$$15° \ 52' \ S \qquad 47° \ 55' \ W$$

'It's a map coordinate!' The words burst out of Jackson's mouth like an involuntary sneeze. He was rewarded for his bizarre behaviour with a burst of laughter from the rest of the room.

'Well, Farley! I was unaware you were such a fan of cartography,' said Crusty, surprised. 'It's a shame your classmates don't share your enthusiasm for maps. Now, settle down, all of you. I'd like three sentences from each of you before the end of the lesson . . .'

Jackson looked excitedly at the coordinates on the whiteboard and then down at the numbers in his palm. Degrees, minutes and seconds, it was the numerical language of navigation. It seemed so obvious to him now; the format was slightly different but, to the young mathematician, the meaning behind the two sets of numbers in his hand was clear: the secret buried by Brooke in her poem was a precise latitudinal and longitudinal map reference.

X marked the spot.

CHAPTER 22

Brooke was bored. She was also cold and damp. But it was the boredom that was really getting to her. It was day three in captivity and she'd read every word of the old newspaper she'd managed to steal from the door pocket of the jet-black, blacked-out Range Rover she'd been bundled into. Thirty-three pages of the *Las Vegas News Herald* by candlelight, by the end of which Brooke decided there ought to be an award for reading it. Most of what hadn't been pulped by the moisture in the mine shaft, where she was being held, had been used by her during toilet breaks. Her captors, two goons with pistols and a seemingly inexhaustible appetite for pizza, allowed her out a couple of times each day to stretch her legs and 'answer the call of nature'.

On the first night, she'd made such a fuss about them watching her that they let her go behind the truck – where she'd reached under the engine block and disconnected an oil pipe. When, next morning, the two chumps discovered an oil slick around the front of their only vehicle, Brooke reminded them of her mechanic's credentials.

'You think I wanna go without food too!' she'd shouted through the wooden barricade behind which she was incarcerated. 'I may have issues with your choice of a pure carbohydrate diet, but I'd rather not starve. Let me take a look at the truck. I'll have her fixed before you can say "pepperoni with three cheeses"!'

And the two fatheads had obliged. They'd watched as their prisoner had spent a few minutes under the big red cruiser, then most of the morning sunbathing on its bonnet while waiting, supposedly, for the rest of the oil to drain. Indeed, they were both extremely impressed when Brooke demonstrated that lamp oil is a perfectly good substitute for engine oil. The only point at which they suspected foul play was when she'd climbed inside the car.

'Easy with the pistolas, boys! I was just makin' sure the lamp oil had done the job,' she said, as at gunpoint, she was frog-marched back to the mine shaft. 'Being as I fixed her up . . .' she added, as they had padlocked her in. 'Any chance one of you oafs could stretch to a salad? I swear I'm gonna barf if I see another dough ball!'

What the heavyset duo didn't know was that the oil change was the final act in an elaborate charade. From the moment the two masked kidnappers had broken into Brooke's garage and seized her where she slept, she had been planning her escape. She may have been blindfolded for the six-hour journey, but that hadn't prevented her from making a couple of critical observations. First, there was the fact that one of her abductors had a working mobile phone. She'd heard him pacing around when they'd stopped for gas and, while she'd failed to catch anything of what was said, the existence of a working mobile phone had been noted. And then there was the voice of Whinin' Wilma, as her dad called her – the sharp tones of the satellite-navigation system that her dull-witted abductors had used to find their way out of Brooke's hometown. They switched off the sound for the last part of the journey, but Brooke knew that a GPS and a mobile phone provided all the technology she needed to broadcast a cry for help.

The first stages of her plan had gone smoothly. The oil scam had given Brooke some precious time in the driver's seat with the electrics on. It took several heart-pounding seconds for the sat-nav to boot up and give her location. As expected, the map itself gave her a big fat nothing. She was truly in the middle of nowhere. But in the time it took the fattest of the two knuckle-heads to notice that the wily young girl had climbed into his vehicle's cabin, then fumble to release himself from his flimsy deck chair, she'd found the two sets of numbers she needed at the bottom of the display.

Brooke had spent the rest of the afternoon in the relative cool of the tunnel, considering how to get her location details to someone useful. She was confident she could get to the mobile phone, but less certain how to use the numbers. After all, she didn't want to take any chances; whoever was behind her kidnapping had managed to bypass the security at her father's ranch. Likely as not, they'd been monitoring her family for a while and there was a chance they still were. If she was going to get her grid reference out, she'd have to be canny about it.

Having meditated on the problem for hours, she gave her tired brain a rest and leafed through what was left of the *Herald*. The last streaks of late afternoon sunlight shone through her slatted prison door to illuminate a grubby crossword on the back page.

Across
9. *Exceptionally talented or intelligent.*

The answer hit her – and not just the answer to the crossword clue. She could substitute the two sets of numbers from the sat-nav for words! And who did she know that could crack that kind of code? Jackson Farley.

Jackson was running late. He jogged down the corridor towards the front entrance to the school and retrieved the sunflowers from the big vase on the front desk where they'd been soaking contentedly for the last few hours. They left a glistening water trail on the polished concrete floor as he hurried towards the glass doors.

On his way out he passed Violet Poole.

'Good luck!' She smiled.

'With what?' Jackson replied.

'Your date?'

'Leave it out,' he replied indignantly as his classmate disappeared through the school doors chuckling.

It was only spitting as Jackson walked outside, but it looked like rain might spoil the rest of the afternoon with his dad – and mum. The thought of it added to his awareness of being outside the safety of school and exposed again.

There was a group of ex-pupils by the school gates, huddled under their hoodies. They were there after school most days and they never normally gave Jackson a second look. But today all four of them seemed to be looking straight at him. *It must be the flowers*, he told himself and hurried away.

The rain had picked up when he reached the high street and Jackson dodged between the shop awnings for cover. Being among the hustle and bustle of the shoppers calmed his nerves slightly. Even so, he was still unnervingly alert to sights and sounds that would normally fail to catch his attention. A stall trader shouted the price of his apples and Jackson anxiously doubled his pace. And then there was the blacked-out Range Rover that cruised past. Had he seen it before?

Away from the high street and up Staffordshire Street, Jackson began running at a pace Mr Spinks, his sports teacher, would have been proud of. Usually Jackson would end up at the back of their monthly PE cross-country runs, or just plain walking with the equally unathletic smokers. Today, however, he ran hard, his rucksack beating out a constant rhythm on the small of his back. He told himself it was so he wouldn't be late for his dad, but there was a good dose of spook in each step, and he checked each junction and crossroads as he ran.

It was about two kilometres to the cemetery. Jackson knew the route well. It was completely out of the way of his route home, but he'd made the massive detour many times. He never went in; that was a privilege reserved for this one day each year. It was enough to just feel close to her, to keep his mum a part of his daily routine.

The rain had been falling in spatters, and Jackson had found its cooling effects on his face quite refreshing. But as he left the shelter of the high street, the rain became a lot heavier, pouring through the tall trees that lined the cemetery.

Jackson's dad was waiting at the entrance, wearing just a thin jacket, but unbothered by the driving rain.

'I won't say you're late, because I don't want to get off on the wrong foot,' he said with a mock scowl. Jackson considered a PE-style excuse, but pulled the sunflowers from inside his blazer instead.

'A bit worse for wear . . . but they'll do,' said Farley Senior, ruffling his son's sopping wet hair.

The cemetery was huge. Almost every patch of the one-hundred-acre site had been allotted a marker. And while the angry rainclouds had turned the rest of the city a gloomy grey, here two whole hillsides dotted with wet granite and glass sparkled as far as the eye could see.

'So, did you do as your mum told you . . . did you *do something you really enjoy* today?'

Jackson thought about how he'd spent half his day trying to solve his friend's kidnapping and the other half terrified that he was next. Far from enjoying himself, he was exhausted, distracted and increasingly jumpy. Even as they walked, Jackson cast cautionary glances at the road that ran alongside the cemetery, any vehicle a shade deeper than light brown causing him palpitations.

He chose not to burden his dad with any of it. This was his problem, and this definitely wasn't the right time.

'Yes . . . I did. I had cheesecake for lunch and I played video games at break.'

'Good lad!' said his dad, as the two made their way

along a narrow gravel path. 'And it's chess club tonight. You love that, right?'

Chess club had completely slipped his mind. All he wanted to do was get back to his computer and see what he could do with Brooke's grid reference.

They walked, past the ranks of angels and straight-faced cherubs, solid stone urns draped in rock cloths and a multitude of photographs in plastic sleeves, of people and pets, some of them twitching in the breeze so they looked alive. But for Alison Anne Farley, there was just an upright slab of steel-blue granite, her name, a date and two uncomplicated words scored into its polished surface. Jackson had wanted to include one of his mum's poems. He kept a notepad full of them in the bottom of his wardrobe. But his dad had informed him the engraver charged by the letter so, in this case, shorter was sweeter. In the end they'd gone with 'Sadly Missed', which, Jackson decided, got straight to the heart of the matter.

They started by clearing the remnants of last year's sunflowers from their metal pot and picking away the leaves. Jackson's dad said a few words about how they both missed her and how he was doing well at work. Then he asked his son if he'd like to have a word on his own, which Jackson knew meant he needed to go off for a few minutes and cry.

'Hi, Mum,' he said, crouching in the wet grass. 'Things

have been a bit hectic. School is good. I've taken up chess – turns out I'm pretty good at it. I think I've managed to get Tyler Hughes off my back. You won't believe how . . .'

He continued to talk, squatting in the rain, recounting the incredible events that had led to him being duped, implicated in robbery on a grand scale and left in fear of his life. But a strange sense of relief came over him as he told his mum everything – the secrets he could never tell anyone else outside MeX. He missed his mum so much.

Mr Farley returned, said a few meaningful words and kissed the top of the wet headstone as he always did at the end of each visit. Jackson looked back at the sunflowers as he and his father walked away. There were plenty of flowers about, but the handful of radiant yellow blooms stood out. *Good choice, Mum.*

Jackson's dad was trying to keep at least one of his promises. He was nattering about the time the three of them had gone camping and he'd forgotten to pack the tent. And the time Mum insisted they try horseriding, which ended with her in hospital thanks to a newly discovered allergy to horses. But Jackson was finding it hard to listen – his thoughts back to finding Brooke and then the twins.

'Well, I think we did it, son. We didn't turn into blubbering idiots,' said Jackson's dad as they reached the gates. 'I promise to eat doughnuts at work tonight and I think you should go and enjoy chess club. It's what Mum would have wanted.'

'But, Dad, I've got so much homework to do.'

His father wasn't interested.

'We gave Mum our word. Now go and enjoy yourself … or you're grounded.' And he pushed a fiver in Jackson's palm and walked away.

CHAPTER 23

'If a game of chess is like a drawn-out tank battle,' declared Willard, 'Bullet Chess is a fast and furious knife fight in a dark alley.' With a quick shuffle, the stringy historian snatched a bishop from his chessboard and thrust it forward like a blade, its black wooden point ending up a millimetre from the nose of Otis Gibbs who sat at the front of the group. Gibbsy, who was just about the smallest boy in school, broke into a broad smile beneath his considerably round spectacles as Willard placed the chess piece-cum-switchblade back on its square, between the knight and the queen.

'One minute thinking time each, for the whole game. That's all you get!'

'One minute? I normally need more than that for one move!' volunteered Olga, the geeky Russian girl whose surname Jackson had never heard pronounced the same twice and hadn't managed to remember yet.

'Yes! And if you're playing it right, if you're digging

deep into your chess-playing soul, it should be more than enough time to mount a murderous assault.'

Jackson wasn't really listening. He sat at the back of the class, his attention on the mobile phone he had surreptitiously switched on. Too much time had passed since he'd extracted Brooke's location from the lines of her poem and he was desperate to find out where they pointed. With the handset's full-colour display glowing in his hands, he stroked his index finger down its touch-sensitive screen until he found a tiny icon that looked like an old-fashioned antenna and poked it. The icon belonged to a program called Terminal Link, which Jackson had downloaded a few months ago. It was supposed to allow anyone with a compatible mobile phone to use their handset to remotely operate their desktop computer. Even with his phone's ability to connect to the Internet, there was little he could do with the longitude and latitude figures from Brooke's poem. But if he could link to the Google Earth program on the computer in his bedroom, he should find where she was being held.

'Farley, what's your favourite chess strategy?' Willard was looking directly at him. Jackson thought how uncanny it was that teachers always chose to single him out when he was trying his best not to be noticed.

Willard's question referred to the chess tactics he had drilled into Jackson and the rest of the club during their run-up to the County Cup. Jackson had found himself obsessed by the legendary formulas of the game of chess. If Willard mentioned a famous 'play', a word used by chess players to describe a series of predetermined moves, Jackson would look it up to study the moves in detail. He'd practise them, playing against himself or online, and committed each play to memory by using algebraic notation.

These famous chess moves had elaborate names: the English Opening, the Elephant Gambit, the Vienna Game – each a clever combination, like a dance routine or a martial arts display. Willard had even concocted his own adaptations of tried and tested chess stratagems which, naturally, he'd given suitably historical handles: Zulu Dawn, Agincourt and one of Jackson's favourite manoeuvres that involved sacrificing his queen, which Willard tagged Queen Boadicea.

'Queen Boadicea,' replied Jackson.

'Well, even the brave queen of the Iceni people would find the pace of a Bullet game frightening,' replied Willard. 'Strategy, you see, requires thought and consideration. But this is different. In Bullet Chess, there's no time for either. Just guts and, hopefully, glory! So, come on, people,' he continued, sitting swiftly down in front of Otis. 'Let's fight!'

Then, in a blur of beige, he punched his side of a

chess timer and moved a pawn directly in front of his bishop, two spaces forward.

There was a clamour of scraping chairs as the other chess clubbers followed suit. The program on Jackson's phone was just loading when Taylor Dillon pulled a chair up to his table. Jackson considered asking him to move on so he could concentrate on his phone, but then he remembered why he was there. *Something you really enjoy.* He had made a promise – he at least had to go through the motions.

Taylor started the game by advancing his white king's pawn two squares. Jackson considered his next move. A procession of practised shapes and patterns rose from the board. If he advanced the pawn in front of his black queen by two squares and could persuade Taylor to take it, then his own queen would be clear to begin the rampage that had won him so many games in the past. Or he could follow up with a knight, or lead his rooks to either side of the board in readiness for an assortment of premeditated pincer attacks.

Taylor coughed politely and the matrix of moves in Jackson's mind vanished. He looked at the clock. So far he'd taken forty seconds and he hadn't moved a single piece.

'Er . . . sorry, Taylor,' he said and simply followed his opponent's lead, pushing his king's pawn forward so the two foot soldiers faced each other in the middle of the board.

Taylor's response was wickedly quick, his queen shooting crossways in readiness for an early charge on Jackson's king.

Jackson considered his answer. It was clear from Taylor's feeble smile and the way he was bouncing his knee up and down that he was gagging for his opponent to get a move on. But Jackson just sat there, pondering the possibilities, while at the same time glancing anxiously from the chessboard to the screen on the phone in his lap. Eventually he placed a hesitant hand on his knight, just as the chess timer started to buzz.

'Taylor wins!' said Willard, who was fresh from demolishing Otis and was watching from the front of the classroom. 'Always remember the clock,' he said, wagging his finger in Jackson's direction. 'You can be one or two moves away from winning with a checkmate, but lose to the clock.'

Jackson could see that Willard wasn't going to let him escape the obligations of being the resident chess-club champ and so was forced to continue playing against a string of opponents who kept arriving at his desk. In the midst of each breakneck battle Jackson furtively entered details to establish a connection with the computer that buzzed away under his desk at home.

By the time the familiar image of his home desktop

had loaded in miniature on his phone's small screen, Jackson had lost three games in a row. His only compensation was the look on Gibbsy's face. His classmate was so delighted to have beaten Jackson that he jumped from his chair and did a little dance, punching the air like a little featherweight boxer. Jackson knew Otis had also been on the wrong side of Tyler Hughes and didn't begrudge him winning something for a change.

Jackson took the opportunity to move the cursor quickly down the screen of his phone, using just a finger. When his nail was hovering over a markedly scaled-down Google Earth symbol, he tapped it and waited impatiently for the program to load.

'You're not playing like the Farley I know.' Willard pulled a chair up to Jackson's table and started setting up the board.

'If you don't mind, Sir, I think I'll sit this one out,' said Jackson, rising from his chair.

'As a matter of fact, I do! Now sit down,' he said firmly. 'Who would have guessed it?' Willard continued. 'Our inimitable champion is slain. Please enlighten us as to why you are playing like you've been flogged with an idiot-stick.'

There were several sniggers from around the room and a look of outright amazement on the face of Otis and Olga who had never heard Willard talk to anyone like that, least of all his golden boy, Farley.

'I'm sorry. I've got things on my mind, Sir.'

'Well then, I suggest you squash them.'

'I'm sorry, Sir?'

'Crush everything but your killer instinct. I told you, this is a different kind of chess game. I know you can think, Farley. The question is, can you fight?' The question hung there between them as Willard whacked his first piece down and thumped the timer.

Jackson was beginning to feel agitated, pushed beyond the limits of his patience, even though he knew Willard was only baiting him. Well, if it was a fight he wanted, then fine.

Jackson made his first move and then, in the split second that Willard's attention was on his own side of the board, Jackson entered the first of the red numbers that stained the inside of his hand into his phone. Willard made his move. Jackson didn't flinch, pushing his piece in an aggressive counter-attack.

As play commenced, Jackson was barely thinking at all, just moving his pieces and secretly entering the map coordinates while his opponent came back at him repeatedly. The two contenders signalled the end of each move with a jab to their side of the chess timer until they were coming in such a blitz that it looked as if they were in danger of pummelling each other. Jackson continued his lightning assault on Willard as he waited for the 3D mapping program on his home computer to return a result to his handset.

Suddenly Willard, who had been swallowing piece after piece of Jackson's most valuable soldiers, realized that he was now confronted by a lowly black pawn, just one square away from his own back row. Jackson had sacrificed his knights, his bishops and his two proud rooks in a fearless march forward.

'I'm promoting my pawn to queen,' said Jackson. It was one of the quirkier rules of the ancient game. Get a humble pawn to your opponent's back row and you can promote him. With two powerful queens now at his disposal, Jackson had Willard's king on the run.

The history teacher stared at the board. He was in a *zugzwang*, a no-win situation, whatever move he made. He knew he was defeated.

Jackson quickly glanced down at his phone. He could see an aerial view of what looked like a range of mountains with a canyon between them. At the top of the screen the word 'Arizona' was written in clear white text and, in the very centre, a small circle representing the precise location of the co-ordinates, just above a town called Mammoth.

'Splendid!' Willard said, with the zeal of someone who had just won, rather than lost. 'That's more like it, my boy. I concede!' And with that he knocked over his king with a spindly forefinger and winked at Jackson.

As Willard walked away, Jackson stared at the fuzzy moonscape of mountains and canyons above the town called Mammoth on his phone's screen. He had found her.

He had found Brooke.

CHAPTER 24

Jackson's tired eyes felt like two dry-roasted nuts. It was only 11 p.m., but it was yet another sleepless night to add to the debt he owed his body. Luckily, his dad had done a shop and there was plenty of chocolate available. He'd get a rap on the knuckles for the missing bars, but they were a crucial part of his strategy to stave off sleep. Strong black tea, toast and chocolate, and the knowledge that Brooke was now in perilous danger were keeping him sharp.

Jackson looked again at the Google Earth program that filled his monitor. From 200 metres up, the desolate hills about Mammoth certainly looked like a candidate for a kidnapper's hideout. He could see from the program's map overlay that there were no main roads nearby and no visible tracks. The assemblage of satellite pictures lacked detail, but it was obvious the area was a ragged collection of boulders, cracks and fissures, the perfect 4x4 off-road challenge, according to one blogger. The only other habitable place that Jackson found in the area was Copper Creek – a deserted mining town he discovered when he zoomed in. According to the web log, the old copper-and-silver mining town was now unreachable by all but the most die-hard off-roaders.

This, according to Brooke's coordinates, was the place. But how could Jackson get there?

Jackson dragged the blog page into line with his own, so both websites – Google Earth and his search screen – were in perfect symmetry. He did this sort of thing when he was deep in thought – laid out pens and pencils equidistantly for exams and made sure his pieces were positioned at the exact centre of each square before an important chess match. Once the mental housework was done, he could focus all of his grey matter on the problem.

He could let Brooke's father, J.P., know of his daughter's location – *he must be worried stupid*. But no matter what assurances he gave, there was no guarantee he wouldn't contact the authorities, and Jackson was sure Lear would be tapped into all official sources. It was unfortunate, because the English family ranch was in California, and couldn't be more than a few hundred kilometres from Brooke's Arizona location. Her father could be there in a few hours, assuming he had access to a 4x4 or . . . *Brooke's Hummer!*

The answer had been in front of him for hours. There were even pictures on the guy's blog showing modified pick-up trucks with colossal tyres and souped-up army vehicles tackling Copper Creek's knotty trails – although Jackson knew they were mere toys compared to Brooke's remotely enhanced vehicle.

Username: GeekSugar. Password: UWill-Nev3rGuess. Jackson had no trouble recalling the login details that Brooke had sent him to access the Hummer's web interface and that had permitted him to rev the vehicle.

He selected the HISTORY tab in his browser's file menu and was offered a list containing every web page he'd visited in the last seven days. They stretched back, like a diary of the last week of Jackson's life, starting with the original search for Elan Drivel and the site that contained MeX's hidden portal, *doyouknowanysecrets.com*. There was the link to Brooke's YouTube video; Jackson's *math-fu* blog. Each link was proof it had all happened. He spotted what he was looking for under 'Friday': 'http://' followed by an incomprehensible collection of letters and numbers, leading to the simple graphical display that would give Jackson remote control of Brooke's two-tonne machine.

The final detail to load was the video feed, a large rectangular black box which filled all of Jackson's twenty-one-inch monitor and over which all the other readouts floated: speedometer, gear-box selector, ignition button. He keyed in his login details and hit ENTER. Nothing changed. His heart sank. If he couldn't rely on Brooke's Hummer, he'd have no choice but to go to the authorities; and Lear, who had already taken his friends, had made clear what the consequences of that action would be.

Then he noticed a faint glow in the jet-black of his flat-panel screen, a soft scarlet speck that wasn't coming from his own reflection.

He leaned forward until his breath was fogging the glass and he could just make out the traces of two or three lacklustre red LEDs. Instantly, Jackson realized that the video feed was live – he was connected to the vehicle! It was just too dark inside Brooke's garage to see anything. Jackson moved his cursor over a small column of buttons on the left of his display and clicked a square labelled LIGHTS. He winced as the garage's whitewashed interior was bathed in the output of six halogen beams. Now he could see the bank of computers that had provided the tiny telltale LEDs.

Jackson could also see the reflection in the mirror at the top of the video display, showing the inside of a firmly closed garage door. In all likelihood there was some clever way of opening it, but Jackson had little time to figure it out and a feeling that one of the US Army's preferred modes of transport wouldn't have any trouble with a bit of wood and aluminium.

The video feed trembled as Jackson clicked the ignition icon and the V8 engine barked itself awake. Next he dragged the small graphic of a gear selector into the REVERSE position and moved the throttle slider halfway up. Jackson barely had time to blink as the Hummer exploded backwards out of the garage and bright sunshine bleached his screen. The high-definition camera behind the vehicle's windshield adjusted to the change in brightness and Jackson saw a Hummer-sized hole in the garage door, which was now about twenty metres in front of him. He decided that if his plan worked, and Brooke was ever free to do so, he'd have her explain the hole to her dad.

The vehicle's rapid exit from the garage had been halted by J.P. English's station wagon, its classic wooden panelling smashed to pieces between the monstrous jeep and the largest pine tree on the ranch. Jackson's headphones emitted an ear-splitting screech and it took a shell-shocked moment before he registered it was the Hummer, still at full revs. He slid the gear stick into PARK and the throttle to ZERO %, then tried to steady his breathing.

This is never going to work, he told himself. *Three hundred kilometres with a mouse for a steering wheel!* Jackson rummaged through his desk drawer, fishing out a small wireless dongle from the snake pit of wires and connectors, along with a PlayStation controller he had modified to within an inch of its life. Then he crawled under the desk to insert the device into the back of his

PC. As he sat back down, Jackson was presented with a close-up view of a middle-aged man in a blue velvet dressing gown and slippers, standing in the driveway and peering inquisitively into the Hummer's camera. Jackson realized he'd just met Brooke's dad.

It hadn't occurred to Jackson that the robotics professor might have something to say about the theft of his daughter's multimillion-dollar machine, but there was no time to think about it.

He thumbed the wireless gamepad's left analogue stick and the vehicle's 500-horsepower engine gave a guttural growl. Professor English jumped back, his eyes wide, as Jackson used his mouse to shift into DRIVE, and his gamepad to wheelspin the high-performance machine down the driveway.

'I'm going to rescue Brooke!' Jackson shouted. It made him feel better, even though the one-way audio system meant Professor English couldn't hear him.

Jackson could see the crumpled remains of the station wagon in the rear-view mirror. There was no way J.P. would be following him in that.

CHAPTER 25

Jackson coaxed the heavyweight robot car northwards. He had left the ornamental ranch gates swinging off their hinges, but now seemed to have the measure of the Hummer and was managing to maintain a steady 60 kilometres per hour. From where he sat, in front of his computer, surrounded by empty chocolate wrappers and console controller in hand, there wasn't a great deal of difference between Brooke's real car and the kind of hotrods he piloted when playing driving games. The whole *driving on the right-hand-side thing* was a little unnerving, but the wide country roads were quite forgiving and Jackson was confident he had cracked his tendency to send the vehicle into the path of oncoming traffic when cornering. His arrival at the first town, however, was a trickier proposition.

The square-nosed 4x4 lurched its way up to the first of several intersections that criss-crossed the busy main street. Jackson had found he could dispense with the mouse and keep both hands on his gamepad. And as long as the throttle stick was full back, the hulking gas-guzzler could be brought to a smooth and solid stop. But accelerating smoothly away from the lights was proving more difficult. However delicately Jackson applied his thumbstick throttle, the seven-litre engine would violently launch the vehicle forward and his attempts to control it merely caused it to bounce and buck its way along the high street. As Hummers went, this H3R was hardly stock; it had been re-engineered to drive itself, and its metallic bodywork was decked with high-tech apparatus. There were five light-detection and ranging scanners, a satellite dish on the roof, and a bank of radar and laser sensors along its front fender, which, all in all, gave it the appearance of a Klingon battle-cruiser. Even for a state accustomed to big ol' cars, *Tin Lizzie* was a bit conspicuous.

Dwight T. Gumption pierced the yokes that sat atop a generous mound of corned-beef hash. Their golden liquid flowed down the sides of the potato and pulped-meat mountain and pooled around the edges of the plate in a way that always reminded Dwight of a volcano. It was his third volcano this week and he had three more to look forward to before his day off. Twelve eggs a week for twenty years; 12,480 in total. *And they ain't done me any harm*, he told himself, while tucking the top of his napkin into his shirt collar and forcing the bottom section between the edge of the table and his stomach. The relish he took in his customary breakfast was sweetened by the fact that Dwight had never paid a penny for it, nor the tankerful of coffee he must have swilled down over the years. And quite right too. He was the Sheriff, after all. If the most important lawman in the county couldn't expect a few perks, then who could?

Sheriff Gumption wiped away the eggy residue that coated his coal-black moustache and squeezed himself out of his favourite booth. Then he swaggered out of the Angry Bear Diner, with a stride he had perfected by watching every John Wayne movie ever made. He would have liked to swing his leg over a horse, but was happy enough with his chrome-plated ride, a Harley Davidson Electra Glide, the prettiest police motorcycle ever made.

As he waited at a stop sign, the air-cooled twin-cam power plant throbbing between his bowed legs, he wasn't sure what annoyed him most about the monstrous vehicle roaring past him. For one thing, it was clodhopping along, stopping and starting its way down Main Street – louder than even Dwight's finely tuned two-cylinder, despite the thunderous exhaust he'd been given at Bob Duke's Custom Cycles by the Duke himself. And this 4x4 was ugly. *Real ugly.* If he had ever watched anything other than westerns, he might have compared it to a Klingon battlecruiser. And, unless the

Sheriff was mistaken, as the *butt ugly* monstrosity twitched and jerked its way past, the driver was so pre-occupied with scrabbling around on the floor with his *CD-multi-changer or some such other newfangled-satellite-powered-doohicky* that he was driving without looking where he was going. He couldn't even see the driver's 'about-to-be-put-in-jail' head. Dwight flicked a switch and lit 'em up.

Jackson noticed the blue flashing lights in his mirror view and what appeared to be one of the Mario Brothers in mirrored shades, riding a motorcycle that under any-one else would have looked massive.

He wasn't quite sure how he was going to handle this one. He could hardly pull over. Chances were, the moment the police officer realized there was no one in the driver's seat he'd radio in, and, assuming J.P. had already raised the alarm, the might of the county's police force would descend on him. The other option of accel-erating away wasn't much more attractive either. If the cop could handle his bike, he'd be impossible to shake.

Jackson reckoned his best bet was a combination of the two.

The officer slid off his mechanical steed and hitched up his belt to show he meant business. The high-def camera that was bolted to the ceiling of the Hummer's cabin had a wide-angle lens and, while it distorted the image of the chubby officer, making him seem even more grotesquely fat as he waddled up to the driver-side door, it enabled Jackson to see him as he peered inside.

Jackson saw the bushy monobrow above the officer's mirrored shades rise as the automatic gear selector slid into the REVERSE position, apparently of its own accord. He could still make out the amazement on the moustached face as the gas pedal depressed itself and the hulking machine shot backwards until its big back tyres rode up and on to the gleaming Harley Davidson with a grinding crunch. Having knocked the vintage machine flat and ground its hand-finished metalwork into the road, the driverless monster lurched forward and sped off, leaving the stupefied lawman at the side of the road.

Relieved, and trying not to laugh too much for fear of crashing, Jackson used Google Earth to navigate away. With a quick snap of the ALT and TAB keys on his keyboard, he was able to switch from his driver's-eye view to the sophisticated 3D program. He had satellite images of the whole planet at his disposal, but all that interested him right now were the few squares of topographical information between his current position and his goal – the abandoned mining town in the Galiuro Mountains. Eventually he'd have to take his chances amid the perilous peaks and gullies that cut off Copper Creek from civilization but, for the next couple of hours at least, he could count on smooth roads and freeways.

The sounds of gunshots rang out before Jackson even noticed the headlamps flashing on the vehicle behind him. He would have preferred a second camera feed from behind, rather than the crudely positioned rear-view mirror. But there was no mistaking the mirrored sunglasses of the man who was driving the absurdly small Fiat 500, barely a centimetre from his rear bumper. It was the Sheriff, one arm out of the window wielding a six-shooter, the other on the teensy car's steering wheel. And by the terrified look on the little old lady's face in the passenger seat, it looked like he truly believed the difference in vehicle size was no barrier to getting his man.

Luckily for Jackson, he'd picked a fight with a county sheriff who was too pig-headed to call for backup. Sheriff T. Gumption had only ever let one perp get away in his long and distinguished career and that was because his trusty bike couldn't float. On that occasion, the runaway jailbird had driven his stolen convertible off a bridge and floated downstream on the white water rapids. Dwight's cousin Willy had found his body a few days later during a fishing trip, but the Sheriff still couldn't chalk him up, on account he had made it over the state line. Now Jackson was dangerously close to crossing into Arizona. And given he'd recently reversed over the Sheriff's motorcycle, which he'd called *Darlin'* and kissed every night before putting to bed, Jackson was in trouble.

The Sheriff was convinced that he'd witnessed some techno-wizardry that enabled the reckless lawbreaker to drive from the back seat, where he'd obviously been hiding, so that he and his homeboys could watch TV or do whatever these rich record-producin', ride-pimpin' Hollywood types did to while away a journey. Jackson checked out the Hummer's rear-view mirror to see if the Sheriff intended to follow up on the initial warning shots. With the same rush of bloodlust that he felt when he and Willy had a deer in their sights, Sheriff T. Gumption raised his handgun and aimed.

The first bullet was deflected through the rear passenger door by its passage through one of the huge batteries that crowded the trunk. Bullet number two ricocheted off the inside of the rear seat and bit a foot-ball-sized chunk out of the front windshield's bottom left corner, taking Brooke's dash-mounted satellite-navigation receiver with it. Jackson's screen didn't register the third metal slug make it through one of the computers, ripping into a circuit board and smashing the main cooling fan.

Jackson was annoyed with himself – he knew he could out-drive a vehicle like this on any driving game.

He pushed the thumbstick and swerved, throwing up rocks that hit the car behind with a satisfying crack of the windscreen. He accelerated hard, leaving the tiny Fiat in his wake and crossing smoothly over the invisible state line into Arizona.

In the Hummer's wake, unnoticed, a line of fuel dripped steadily from the hole made in the fuel line by the final bullet.

CHAPTER 26

The dark, humid bedroom, together with Jackson's hunger and lack of sleep, had made his driving dangerously erratic. To avoid any unwanted attention that an unmanned Hummer might attract, Jackson knew he needed to be much more alert.

His wireless controller at least allowed him to stretch his legs. He wasn't about to test its range, but knew he could move safely within the boundary set by his desk and bed. He set the Hummer to cruise at a conservative 60 on the freeway and managed to reach out and poke his bedroom window open. He drank in the warm night air, its oxygen and sour city scents sparking his second wind. He poured the dregs of every Coke can he'd ever failed to bin down his parched throat, and tentatively revisited a pack of biscuits he'd lost behind his computer sometime last year. Soon his display was showing the town of Mammoth and the small road that branched north-east, towards Copper Creek.

There were no other vehicles on the road, and Jackson

was thankful for that as now his navigational skills were being tested. He was covering the throttle and steering with one hand, while switching between the car's video feed and the 3D map with the other. Within a few kilometres the trees thinned and the road began to narrow until it was little more than a footpath. The aerial pictures that had guided him here showed little more than pixellated rock patterns between the end of the road and the point that marked Brooke's location. All Jackson could do was point the vehicle in the general direction of the abandoned town and hope for the best.

After some time, the Hummer crested a rough-hewn plateau and Jackson caught a glimpse of the shimmering canyon. He could almost feel the heat coming off the searing landscape beyond his computer screen as the off-roader tore down the next poor excuse for a track. Each stone and pothole shook the suspension as the beast of a vehicle spat them out. Then the barely visible trail vanished altogether, and the car was rolling down a steep incline. Jackson carefully applied some back pressure to his controller's left thumbstick. But the brakes failed to bite – the vehicle just kept on rolling.

His first thought was that his gamepad had malfunctioned, but he still had steering and the engine growled as impressively as ever when he tried the throttle. But without brakes, the machine was in virtual free fall down a steep slope of loose grit and shingle.

There was nothing Jackson could do.

Prison has its advantages, pondered Brooke. *At least if I were in jail, as opposed to cooped up in this filthy hole like a rat, I could ask to be let out on a chain-gang.* It was proof of Brooke's desperation that breaking rocks with a pick-axe all day would be considered an improvement. She had considered applying similar muscle to the walls of her cell. But her engineer's experience told her the hundred-year-old joists keeping the air shaft open were looking for an excuse to retire, so any efforts in that direction were likely to leave her buried alive in silt and copper.

Worse than thoughts of cave-ins were the titan-like proportions Brooke's imagination had given to the critters that shared her hole. She was no scaredy-cat. Life on the ranch brought its own share of snakes, scorpions and bugs, but, like the rest of the population of California, they were too busy relaxing in the Sunshine State's perfect climate to go around getting angry and biting folks. But this was Arizona – the devil's own blacksmith's forge, with Death Valley, the hottest place on Earth, down the road somewhere, and heat this fierce made everything mad as hell. Something stirred in the back of the cave. A rat? A bat? A jackrabbit? Or was it the sound of something more deadly? Brooke started to shout.

Shouting, Brooke had discovered, was her one guaranteed method of ruining her captors' day. For the two hired hoods guarding her, this was quite a cushy job. They had a tent each, and a barbecue – if they felt inclined to spice up their daily intake of pizza – with an amply loud satellite radio, care of their truck. All things considered, they had enjoyed three days of sunbathing, cook-outs and heavy-rock classics. The latter wasn't their first choice. If truth be known, both men would much rather have listened to sport. Indeed, the quieter of the two men hid a penchant for classical music and had found it difficult these past few nights not to give away his secret by loud humming as the majesty of the night sky out here filled his head with Gustav Holst and Chopin. Tuning to a heavy-rock station was their only way of drowning out Brooke's wailing banshee act.

Brooke was screaming now and, in the opinion of the quiet man, it was a pitch somewhere between a soprano saxophone and the top 'A' from Elgar's Cello Concerto. The reason for the screeching was harder to discern, so he walked over to the wooden staves that he himself had used to turn the entrance to the ancient mine shaft into a jail. He was good with his hands and would have liked to follow in his grandfather's footsteps and become a carpenter. But there were other ways of making money from strong hands and fists and, where he came from, it was hard to resist easy money.

As he leaned down to peer inside, two eyes looked out of the darkness like a tiny set of headlamps and a scrawny hand shot out and grabbed him by the forearm.

'There's something in here,' the girl declared angrily. 'You can either come in and get it, or give me your flashlight and let me deal with it. But while you make your decision, I'm gonna keep on screamin'.'

From this close up, the sound the girl could make was ear-splitting. No way was he going in there. He pulled the Maglight from his belt and placed it in a gap between two pieces of wood before the cold metal tube was snatched inside.

After rooting behind the pallets and rusted oil drums stacked against the rock wall sealing the shaft, Brooke found the cause of her concern. A family of dormice were caught in the flashlight's beam, a mother and at least four babies in a nest of twigs and chewed shreds of plastic. Brooke smiled. 'Well, ain't you as cute as a bug's ear?' she said, carefully placing a thin sliver of wood over her fellow prisoners.

She walked back to the tunnel entrance and was about to start winding up the man who waited for his torch, when she noticed the unmistakable outline of *Tin Lizzie* coming down the slope above the camp. Realizing she needed to conceal the sound of its approach, Brooke acted fast.

She started screaming.

To Jackson's astonishment, the Hummer was still on its wheels, despite a section of incline so steep that it could only have been one or two degrees off vertical. Having eased off the throttle completely, the speedometer was still showing 60 kmph, which now seemed pretty unnerving. With no sign of the brakes working, the car hurtled downwards to the first crumbling ruins of the old town.

The Hummer took the side clean off the first roofless shell of a building that got in its way, and continued to bound over the tiers cut into the canyon as the slope smoothed out. Then Jackson spotted two bright blue tents and a jet-black Range Rover on a small patch of scrubland beyond his bonnet. The high-speed 4x4 reached the camp in a matter of seconds and, swerving to avoid the tents, he aimed the machine at the softest-looking part of the rock face in front of him.

Brooke instantly computed the speed of the incoming vehicle and realized it had run out of stopping distance. She dived backwards as the wooden gates of her jail exploded, covering her with chunks of timber and rock. The bull-bars on the front of the Hummer smashed through the sturdy wooden front of the mine, leaving the shiny nose of the vehicle buried inside the cave, like a faithful dog sniffing out its owner. Suddenly the ancient timbers began to buckle, sending a cloud of dust rolling towards her. Instinctively scooping up the tiny nest of brown mice, Brooke sprinted towards the light, blindly leaping on to the bonnet of her car.

Jackson had expected to see either a blank screen or a burning inferno of twisted Hummer parts. Instead Brooke's filthy face filled his screen and one word boomed in his headphones: 'Drive!'

Fumbling for his mouse, he dragged the on-screen gear shift into REVERSE, throwing the Hummer backwards through two tents and a barbecue and into the side of a Range Rover. He slipped into DRIVE, applied the throttle to maintain traction, and launched the car towards the only available exit, almost turning one of Brooke's captors into road-kill.

Despite being terrified by the responsibility he held in his palm, Jackson was grateful to be this side of the controls. If the route into the valley had been bad, the route out was a virtual rock-and-boulder theme park. The valley floor was fat with stones from a few thousand years' landslides and Brooke bounced over every one of them.

And now the bullets started. No match for the Hummer's speed, the black Range Rover chasing Brooke made short work of any obstacles the valley threw at it. And at every smooth patch its driver sprayed a volley of slugs at the Hummer.

Jackson knew Brooke's machine could only sustain so many hits. He changed direction, the Hummer veering violently off the valley floor and up a steep slope. Brooke clung desperately to her windshield wiper handholds as *Tin Lizzie* tore up the slope, sliding round the gravelled edges of sheer drops and certain death.

From his dingy room in south London, Jackson could have been forgiven for thinking he was looking at the surface of Mars. The precision optics that fed his high-definition video stream offered a glorious panorama of the hard-baked wilds of the Grand Canyon State. And he could see that despite a hairy downhill section to negotiate, with a few lowland dips and bumps, the road to Mammoth was tantalizingly close. Better still, they seemed to have lost the black Range Rover.

As the battered Hummer coasted momentarily on the smooth plateau, Brooke took the opportunity to clamber from the hood to the roof and, stretching a slender arm down to the door handle, managed to swing the front passenger door open and flop uncomfortably inside. Her wild face appeared immediately in front of Jackson's view.

'Back off the hammer, daddy-o!' said Brooke through the dust and the cracks on the windshield. 'You're doin' good, but you might want to think about using the anchors!' Jackson desperately wanted to tell his friend that, for reasons unknown, the brakes on her car were shot. But, as they both knew, the Hummer's communication system was one-way. Besides, Jackson was confident he could cruise the machine down the steep incline by using the gear shifter to limit its speed. He blipped the throttle stick and slipped into second as the robust vehicle rocked forward and started to trundle quickly downhill.

'Unbelievable!' Jackson spun round in shock at the sudden interruption. His dad stood in the door of his room.

'A driving game . . . at five in the morning! Turn it off!'

'But, Dad –'

'Turn it off now!'

Jackson turned reluctantly to the screen and in one swift motion moved his cursor up. He clicked on the bright red AUTO-DRIVE button in the Hummer's graphics overlay and switched his monitor off.

'If I hear a sound coming from your room, you won't know what's hit you, young man,' his dad fumed. 'When you get up . . . in just over two hours . . . you and I are going to have a serious chat about you and your computer use.'

And Jackson had to climb into his bed and close his eyes.

CHAPTER 27

Brooke didn't know it yet, but as *Tin Lizzie* hastened down the slope towards the first of several sharp bends, her fate was in the hands of a few thousand lines of code. The Hummer's brain, made up of three networked computers on the back seat that were still working, was using the perpetual logic of algorithms – problem-solving operations begged, borrowed and stolen from her father – to make sense of the flood of information flowing from banks of sensors all over the vehicle's body. The Hummer could 'see' the sheer drop at the edge of the approaching corner and computed that at this speed, with this much weight, on these road conditions, with these tyres at this tyre pressure and with this amount of compression in the suspension, and in this gear . . . it had better slow down.

Brooke did her instinctive calculations in a fraction of the time it took her mechanical creation to come to the same conclusion and went to her own default response for such situations. She started to scream.

'Slow down! Put the goddam brakes on!'

But the Hummer, still computing, carried on charging towards the bend. Its terrified passenger struggled to strap herself into the three-point harness her mother had made her install, but which she had never wanted to use until this moment. Brooke wiped the sweat from her brow, her eyes fixed on the brake pedal and its heavy pneumatic coupling which clearly weren't moving. *This is it, cowgirl. Your luck is up. You are going to die*, said a voice in Brooke's head that she didn't want to believe but had to admit was probably right. All that stood between the Hummer and a few hundred metres of fresh air was a thin trail that clung to the mountainside. Brooke closed her eyes and prepared for the Hummer's first and only attempt at flight.

She thought she felt the vehicle start to drift sideways. Her eyes shot down. She certainly wasn't dead yet. The Hummer's gear-shifter was darting up and down, moving between its various positions at breakneck speed. Both back wheels swung out to the very edge of the track as the boxy four-wheel drive used every molecule of dirt and soil available to keep itself upright.

Tin Lizzie made it round the corner with a millimetre to spare. As the Hummer prepared for two more hairpin bends, Brooke stared at the glowing AUTO-DRIVE indicator on the dashboard. A broad and very relieved smile spread across her face. She wasn't sure why the brakes had failed or why Jackson had obviously turned the controls over to *Lizzie*, but she was certain of one thing. The problem with *Lizzie*'s steering that had been dogging her for months was solved – and the car had saved her life.

Without the brakes, the auto-drive mechanism was better able to keep the vehicle stable. Altering the algorithm in favour of traction during cornering was the key. She had been too concerned with stopping. Ease off on the brakes side of the equation . . . and *Lizzie* would be a better driver. Brooke had Sheriff Dwight T. Gumption to thank for the *eureka* moment in the development of her self-driving car. His fourth bullet had entered one of the computers that, among other duties, was responsible for braking.

Less impressive, however, was the fact that *Lizzie* seemed to be haemorrhaging gasoline. Brooke was unaware of the bullet that caused it, but very aware that once her engine stopped, even *Lizzie*'s bootload of batteries could only keep her robot brain alive for a few minutes. Without juice, she'd be a fast-moving lump of scrap metal.

A deathbed on wheels for Brooke.

Mr Farley had been in the bathroom for ages. Given that he still had to walk past Jackson's room in prison-guard mode, get back into bed and go through his usual five-minute cooling-down period during which – as Jackson knew from bitter experience – he would have increased hearing sensitivity, Jackson was looking at ten whole minutes before he could get back in front of his computer.

He tried his hardest to block the terrifying picture of Brooke speeding off a cliff and felt sick. Straining his ears for sounds from his dad's end of the flat, Jackson hoped the silence meant he had fallen asleep. As he powered up his monitor, Jackson prayed there was something and someone left to drive.

'I don't know where you been joyridin', Jackson, but you've done used up all her motion lotion.'

Jackson couldn't have been more relieved to see both Brooke and *Tin Lizzie* still in one piece, but was very alarmed to see the fuel gauge now showing empty. But that wasn't the worst of it. The outline of the black Range Rover was back in the centre of the Hummer's mirror.

Brooke poked her head into the camera lens; Jackson could see that the fight had gone from her. 'You done good, partner, but you better pull her over while we still can.'

Jackson steered the Hummer on to a smooth patch of dirt at the side of the road as it rolled to a stop. He expected to see his gutsy friend leap from the car and run for the hills, but instead she slowly unclipped her harness and walked round the front of the car.

'Tell my mum and dad I'll be OK,' she said, staring straight into the windshield. 'Tell 'em . . . that I'll figure a way out of this . . . somehow.'

But Jackson wasn't listening. In fact, he was trying to stop himself bellowing at the computer screen. In the distance, coming round the corner, was an armada of blue flashing lights, assorted pick-ups and bob-tailed trucks, all led by the tiny Fiat 500 that had almost ended Jackson's rescue attempt several hours ago. He checked the Hummer's mirror again just in time to see the Range Rover kicking up a cloud of dirt as it performed a hasty about-face. When the dirt settled, it was nowhere to be seen.

Brooke had heard the growing cacophony of engines behind her and turned to see the curious convoy approaching. She took two paces forward, then stopped and turned back.

'This isn't over, cowboy. We need to finish this. Be ready!' Then she smiled at him with a warmth that if anyone had witnessed it, would have made Jackson blush.

CHAPTER 28

The plan, according to Brooke, was simple. Borrow two asteroid mining robots, fly them halfway around the world to gather damning evidence of Lear's Ukrainian operation, then use it to bargain for the release of the Kojimas and ultimately bring Lear to justice. Jackson had wanted to laugh out loud – except that he dare not incur the wrath of the feisty engineer.

235

It was the kind of plan that only Brooke could dream up. But, to be fair, Jackson thought the idea was no more outlandish than the past week's events. And besides, what choice did they have? So, in the space of just half an hour, Brooke had managed to take Jackson through an extraordinary range of topics, including orbital velocity, low Earth orbit, drag force and her father's patented two-stage heat shield that could withstand 2,700 degrees Fahrenheit – which, according to Brooke, who Jackson was quite positive had just set a world speed-talking record, was hot enough to melt rock. But his American teammate had saved the best bit until last – the bit that involved him piloting one of the two experimental robots.

Brooke's father was planning to send two small robotic mining machines into space from a private launch facility in California. They would complete a single orbit around Earth, before dropping down to the Mojave Desert where an audience of Chinese investors could witness first hand the short work their prototype tools could make of the rocky desert floor. And Brooke would be at Professor J. P. English's side. She was, after all, the best operator he had and she was the brains behind many of the systems he would be testing. Also, he and the police still hadn't managed to get to the bottom of her mysterious kidnapping and her father was afraid to let Brooke out of his sight.

While Brooke's crash course in astrophysics was a little quick even for Jackson's mathematical brain, he was clear about his role. Assuming their makeshift machines made it to the Ukraine, it was Jackson's job to work out exactly where they'd find Lear's gang. Lear's whole operation was designed to be mobile so, if Jackson and Brooke were going to gather the evidence that would bring Lear to justice, they needed to be sure where it was.

Jackson had also been tasked with sourcing the parts to build himself a hand-held controller for one of the asteroid robots which Brooke had called *Tug*. It could be any controller he wanted, but it needed to connect to an enhanced version of *Tin Lizzie*'s online interface that Brooke was working on. Jackson knew just where to start.

According to the tag line on the sign above the steps, 'Nick's Nax' was 'an emporium of the pre-owned'. The tardis of a place was accessed by a narrow stairwell, and occupied a single storey above a piano shop. It smelled like a museum, but had none of the orderliness. The muddled merchandise was bundled on racks under handwritten signs for things like metal detectors, turntables and disco lighting, but which rarely described what was found beneath them. In the centre of the shop was a full-sized jet-ski which was straddled by a mannequin wearing what appeared to be a green Darth Vader costume. Jackson had enquired about the outfit and been told it was a chemical warfare suit which had been traded in by a soldier just home from Iraq. He wasn't sure whether that was true, but it was pretty cool.

The gaming section of the shop was near the till. Behind it was the owner, Nick, whose almost total lack of hair made him appear ageless, moaning loudly about how much stuff had been stolen from his chock-a-block shelves. He raised his voice so a small boy in the Retro Games section could hear him. 'You'd need a time machine to be able to play some of that stuff,' he said to Jackson, while keeping one eye on the boy. 'You'd think he'd prefer to go into town and thieve games that aren't one up from cave drawings.'

'I guess so,' Jackson replied noncommittally.

'He'll get a shock if he makes a run for it,' Nick continued. 'I've got a new security measure.' He pulled out something round and shiny from underneath his desk. 'Throwing star! A guy swapped it for three games and a web cam. Which I swear he nicked off me last Tuesday.'

The object in Nick's hand was indeed a fine example of the ancient Japanese hand-launched weapon. Jackson marvelled at the ornate decoration on its five razor-edged blades.

'Isn't that a bit over the top?'

'It certainly is not! I figure I only need to stick one kid with it and word will get round.'

Jackson wasn't sure if Nick was being serious, but thought it best he get down to business.

'I'm after a new Nintendo controller.'

From the specifications that Brooke had emailed over, it was clear that his PlayStation gamepad wouldn't do the job. For starters, it didn't have enough functions to cover all of Brooke's requested parameters, and while many gamers swore by the feel of its analogue sticks, Jackson had always preferred the freedom offered by fully programmable digital controls. What he really wanted to use was the MeX fountain pen. The stubby blue writing instrument was the most unlikely joystick, but he would have hacked what lay inside its plastic shell – if he could. Jackson suspected that an array of microscopic accelerometers and digital compasses gave the futuristic interface its almost wand-like quality, but he couldn't be sure. And if he opened it up, he risked wasting what little time he had. The nearest approximation of Lear's technology that the young gamer could think of was the wireless controller from Nintendo.

'And what makes you think I've got one of them?' The crafty owner was being tactically evasive. Jackson had stood in front of this counter enough times to know this was all part of the shop owner's idea of his role as a modern version of a medieval merchant. Jackson knew, as most regulars did, that Nick had as much new kit out the back as he had crusty old relics in the front.

'And assuming I have said goods, what would you be willing to barter?'

Jackson carefully pulled from his backpack a fist-sized object wrapped in a duster and handed it to Nick. He opened the yellow cloth with an Egyptologist's reverence and held the statuette of Buffy up to the light.

'A rare and mystic treasure,' Nick agreed admiringly. Then, remembering how his enthusiasm often got in the way of his haggling, added, 'You sure you didn't nab this from me last month?'

'No, I did not!'

'Of course, she would be far more enchanting were you able to stretch to a sweetener.'

Jackson was prepared. He dug deep into his trouser pocket and then placed four pound coins on the counter one by one.

'Uh huh . . .' said Nick expectantly.

Jackson placed another pound on the table . . . and when the man's silence became unbearable, one last coin.

'Congratulations, you have yourself a deal,' said Nick, loping towards the store room. 'Keep an eye on that little scoundrel.'

Jackson locked eyes with the tiny boy. Without breaking his gaze, the young lad extended a scrawny arm from inside a long coat at least two sizes too big for him. Having grabbed a handful of ancient games in cardboard sleeves, he stuffed them inside the coat and nonchalantly carried on browsing. Jackson thought about the five-bladed ancient Japanese weapon and said nothing.

Jackson's room was untidy at the best of times. It had been variously compared by his unamused dad to a cesspit, a tramp's hovel and, perhaps most accurately, a black hole, meaning a place where things enter but never exit. As part of his penance for his 5 a.m. 'driving-game' session, a no-gaming-on-a-school-night offence,

Jackson had agreed to straighten up his room. He had also agreed to make his dad's sandwiches on his return from school each afternoon. But after one night shift with a squishy cellophane-wrapped preparation of peanut butter, honey and grated cheese, Farley Senior had let his son off that one.

After the big clear-up operation, Jackson's room had remained relatively shipshape for about a day, but over the course of the week had descended to new depths as a miscellany of electronic components for the asteroid-mining robot controller appeared on every available surface. Hopefully, his planned modifications for the new wireless controller would succeed where the insides of several joysticks and keyboards had failed.

He carefully removed the thin plastic shell of the controller and, using a scalpel, levered up the wafer-thin printed circuit board inside. Its microscopic components sat like tiny towns and villages on a little green glen.

Jackson then located the 'voodoo' in the cheap controller: the minuscule motion sensors, tiny silicon machines, each a feather-light mechanical contraption capable of translating every waggle of the modern magician's wand into the subtle mathematics of movement. He scooped out the fragile innards and cleared them a space on his desk. Next, he used small sections of wiring to connect a couple of AA batteries inline with the naked gadget's power connectors. Two tiny lights came on, and the rectangular skeleton was alive.

Jackson's bedroom surgery remained open for many more hours, as he refined the wireless connection between the electronic guts on his desk and his PC, using various software programs he had downloaded. The final stage of the operation involved carefully removing the tubular blade from his cherished replica lightsabre. It was the second of his most valued treasures to be sacrificed and there could be no finer proof of Jackson's commitment to bringing Lear down and rescuing his teammates. Opening up its hilt, Jackson was able to transplant the bare circuit board and batteries inside the narrow metal handle.

The finished instrument was fit for a Jedi Master. It was heavier than it looked and its stripped rubber grip stuck to the meat of his palm. There were eight fully operational buttons drilled in two lines along its body, and, as its enthusiastic inventor wielded it like a rapier, his every twist and thrust was picked up as pixel-perfect inputs by the test software on his monitor.

The converted movie prop may have had a touch of the Hollywood about it, but there was nothing make-believe about its intended use. Jackson's mind drifted to the mountains of Ukraine, where he saw the ruined village and its destitute inhabitants. He had been constantly on edge since Brooke's rescue and every time he thought he saw a blacked-out Range Rover, or a potential kidnapper in every passer-by, it made him more determined to find Lear and finish this.

CHAPTER 29

'Now? Whatcha mean *now*?' said Jackson from the cafe, trying to keep the ketchup from running down the sleeve of his triple-decker bacon sandwich hand.

'It's hard to speak,' said Brooke in a whisper. 'But I'm at the launch facility and we're minutes away from countdown.'

'Would it have killed you to give me half an hour's warning?' said Jackson, stuffing the whole sandwich into his mouth in one go and looking for somewhere to wipe his hand before settling for the tablecloth.

'The investors were beginning to get cold feet and Dad decided to go straight ahead with the launch. I've sent the login details to your email,' she hissed. 'Just get your bed-wallowin' behind back home.'

So much for a relaxing Saturday breakfast, thought Jackson, as he limped breathlessly into the block of flats after running all the way. He looked up to see the lift doors taped shut and a big OUT OF ORDER sign hanging above them. Of all the times for them to fail, it had to happen now. Jackson already felt nauseous after eating too quickly, then running too fast. Now he faced eighteen flights of stairs. He put the first four floors behind him with little trouble, but by the fifth he could taste bacon again, mixed with mucus. About halfway up, stopping to catch his breath, he decided that perhaps he would try harder for Spinks in the next cross-country. Even the smokers would have made it up the stairwell quicker than he could right now.

The two men in the launch room, blissfully ignorant of Brooke's alternative plan for their very expensive robots, were the facility's launch director who squinted at her through remarkably dense spectacles whenever he spoke, and Nathaniel Goulman, a shy but brilliant PhD student who had hung around after graduating from Professor English's class and had become an indispensable part of his many projects. He worked mainly with J.P. on the university campus in Massachusetts and his considerable skills in the discipline of computer science came a close second to those of the great man himself. It also helped that Goulman was an obsessive body builder. In light of recent events, J.P. found it reassuring that the systems analyst for this test flight could benchpress 315 pounds.

The operations room was built inside a bombproof bunker. For its three inhabitants, who were working in close proximity to a launch vehicle filled with over one million litres of liquid hydrogen and liquid oxygen, its one-metre thick concrete walls and blast-resistant steel doors were reassuring. The room itself was packed with computers and flat screens; and, after J.P. had insisted on adding his own gear, there was barely room to walk between workstations.

Brooke looked up at her father on a large monitor above her terminal.

'Have you fixed it yet?' J.P.'s face loomed large. Brooke had already managed to delay lift-off for a few minutes by stringing a line about possible loss of pressure in one of the cryogenics tanks. A system for pumping frigid gases around the launch vehicle's main stage was required to keep its liquid fuels cold enough to prevent them exploding as they sat there. The system was functioning perfectly, but Brooke knew it was just the thing to buy her some time. Now that time was just about used up. The launch window, a combination of weather conditions and the precise prediction of where certain lethal chunks of orbital debris would be, was about to close. She would have to give the thumbs-up for the automated start sequence in the next sixty seconds, or not at all. But where on earth was Jackson?

Brooke wiped the sweat from her top lip and stared at the launch vehicle, which sat quivering in a heat haze on her screen. Its largest component was its fuel tank. The fat white tube towered thirty metres above the ground, two shorter solid booster rockets strapped to its sides like an afterthought. Sunk partly in a deep trench was the main engine, designed to drink an explosive cocktail of liquids from the fuel tank, then spew them out in a fiery stream that would push the whole assembly into low Earth orbit. Then the bright white phoenix would die, leaving nothing but a tiny capsule in the silence of space from which J.P.'s robot brood would hatch.

'Go for auto-sequence start ... T minus thirty seconds . . .' said the director from the terminal across from Brooke. The young engineer was sure of one thing: if her British friend didn't arrive soon, it would be impossible to patch him into the complex communications system without someone noticing. And the only chance of getting Lear would be lost.

Jackson's chest was still heaving and his nose was wet. Even his teeth and gums hurt. All the same, he had made it. The computer hummed happily under his desk, but his online email was being painfully slow. After what seemed like enough time to run up and down the stairs all over again, but was really only ten seconds, a list of new messages appeared, including one from Brooke. Jackson clicked on the web link in Brooke's mail and a page not unlike *Tin Lizzie*'s appeared. It looked like a mash-up of the Hummer's web interface and the screen from a flight simulator. Jackson could see the familiar USERNAME and PASSWORD fields, but in place of the car's speedometer and gear-shift graphics there were several simple, line-drawn gauges. Labelled THRUST and BATTERY, they had a cluster of indicators with eye-catching titles – GRENADE, CLAW, MAGNET and SHUNT – overlaid on the black background of the video feed. There was also a faint emerald-green circle in the top left, which Jackson assumed was some form of navigational display, given the '20 km' that was written beneath it.

He entered the necessary details and waited.

'T minus twelve seconds and counting . . .' announced the launch director, reading from a screen full of digits.

'Good luck, guys,' said Brooke's father. She could see him standing in the desert with a bunch of small men in grey suits, hiding behind binoculars and telescopes.

'12 . . . 11 . . .'

Where are you, Farley?

'10, 9, 8, 7, 6 . . . Main engine's start.'

A bright white LED flashed up at Brooke's workstation. Jackson. She sighed in relief.

'Problem?' asked Mr Goulman.

'Negative. Got it covered,' Brooke said, quickly clicking to accept the incoming comms request.

'3, 2, 1 . . . Booster ignition and lift-off!'

All the video feeds from the launch pad greyed out as a wave of smoke and steam engulfed the structure. The building that housed Brooke and her two colleagues was a good fifty metres away, but as the spacecraft was propelled skywards, the pressure wave from its powerful engines hit their building and every display, rack and mounting rattled.

'Nice of you to join us,' Brooke said quietly into her microphone.

'I thought showing up late for a gig was considered rock 'n' roll!'

The twelve deck chairs were, literally, in the middle of nowhere. Each one had its own cooler beside it, containing a bottle of champagne and several bottles of water. And each chair was occupied by a man in a suit.

'If you look to your monitors now, you should see the main fuel stage falling away,' said Professor English, wiping sweat from his face with a handkerchief. He cut a romantic figure against the flat sandy landscape with its mountainous backdrop. With his leather flying jacket, white silk scarf and quiff of jet-black pomaded hair, he looked more like a Second World War flying ace than a distinguished academic.

As each man stared into the small LCD screen in

their hand,' J.P. continued. 'It will follow the same path as the solid booster rockets and fall to the west of Mojave, with assistance from drogue and main parachutes. A beacon will guide our recovery crew to its location. In a few minutes' time the remaining capsule will establish itself in orbit, after which our flight director will hand over the mission to the engineer in charge of the deployment stage – my daughter, Brooke English.'

When they heard Brooke's name, the men bowed and applauded enthusiastically.

'He certainly knows how to put on a show,' murmured Jackson. 'I'm assuming you haven't told your dad what we intend to do with his precious cargo?'

'I think it's best if we don't dwell on that.' Brooke tried to bury her guilty thoughts. Since her return, her father had made a real effort. He'd cancelled a couple of meetings up in Boston, and the three of them had even sat round the kitchen table and eaten as a family. They hadn't done that since Christmas.

To distract herself, Brooke thought about the problem of her two colleagues in the room. She wouldn't get much past them, with them sitting so near, and they surely wouldn't let her hijack the mission. She had a diversionary tactic, but would it work? She had exactly forty minutes to find out. Just under half the duration of the orbit that J.P. was now explaining to his guests.

The precise amount of time it would take the capsule, currently 300 kilometres above them, to reach Eastern Europe.

CHAPTER 30

'I need to speak to you urgently, J.P.!' The desperation in Mr Goulman's voice was apparent, even over the static of the two-way radio.

'What is it? Why are you speaking to me on the radio?' said Professor English.

'The launch director and I are standing outside the operations room.'

'I'm sorry, I don't follow!'

'It's your daughter, J.P. . . . she's locked us out!'

Inside the cramped operations room, Brooke was grinning at how easy it had been to get her two co-workers to leave the bunker. Setting the fire alarm off was easy, and she'd never seen anyone move so quickly as she screamed out, 'Fire! Fire! Fire!' Then she just got up, closed the reinforced door behind them and sat back down.

But it was time to be serious now.

'How's that joystick of yours coming along?' she asked Jackson.

'It's not exactly a joystick...' replied Jackson, holding the modified lightsabre in his hand. It had been easier than he expected. After pairing it up with his computer, he'd simply assigned a few commands from Brooke's web page to the buttons. 'I wouldn't have minded a practice.'

'I'll tell you everything you need to know on the way in. But for now, just sit back and cross your fingers. Initiating Descent Phase.'

Two fireballs streaked a path through Earth's upper atmosphere before the re-entry computer gave the command to shed the charred carbon plating that made up the first-stage heat-shields. Then what their originator, Professor English, described as two 'large black air-bags' ballooned out around each machine, at once slowing their descent, and acting like big beach balls on touchdown.

Jackson's machine, the one Brooke had referred to as *Tug*, bounced clean over a farmhouse, before taking the top two layers off a stone wall and burying itself in the side of a metal grain silo. The final act of the computer that had controlled every stage of *Tug*'s descent was to vent the gas inside the tough polyethylene-plastic ball that surrounded the robot. As the wedge-shaped robot sparked into life, Jackson flexed his fingers nervously round the metal shaft of his wireless stick, ready to take over.

*

Kostya had been walking these hills since he was a child. His pace had slowed in the last few years, but he was limber enough to make it to his favourite spot before the sun sank behind the mountains.

The first thing the old man noticed was a noise from Olena's farm. It was a tinny crunch like a car being crushed and it didn't belong out here, a hundred kilometres from the nearest breaker's yard. It wasn't easy to see from on top of the hills – it wasn't easy to see anything at his age – but he would swear that the tin grain-tower was leaning over. Had it always been like that, or was he just getting old and forgetful? Still, it was a strange thing, an enormous grain-tower as crooked as a wizard's hat.

The next sound to reach the elderly herdsman was like a boar charging towards him through the trees. He'd seen a few in his time. He'd shot one once and sold what he couldn't eat. The noise grew louder, rumbling and crashing through the trees until something broke clear of the thicket – something big and black that was rolling towards him.

Kostya felt once more like the scared thirteen-year-old boy who had faced the German Army in Odessa all those years before. He would have liked to run and hide from the huge black cannonball, but his old bones wouldn't allow it, so instead he just stood in the tall grass as it rolled to a stop a few metres from him. Nothing was stranger than what happened next, and nothing more was necessary to convince the old Red Army soldier that the Nazis were back. Kostya instinctively ducked at the suppressed cracks that sounded just like shots from a *Sturmgewehr* rifle. Then the matt-black ball, which stood taller than the old man stooped, opened up – and a smaller ball rolled out. The dull metallic sphere propelled itself along the ground by spikes that stuck out and retracted from points all over its skin, so that it made a kind of fluttering sound. The Nazi contraption completed its metamorphosis by sprouting three stubby rotor blades and taking to the air. The whining sound it made put the startled old man in mind of the noise the shells made when he had last stood at the mercy of the German war machine. What could he do but watch as the strange sphere disappeared into the valley? He couldn't run and raise the alarm. Even if he still had a rifle, his arthritic hands couldn't hold it steady. He wasn't sure, but he thought his old eyes were showing him a second machine. This one, triangular-shaped, joined up with the floating metal ball and headed across the field below.

So be it. If this was the start of another invasion or perhaps the beginnings of lunacy – it was only to be expected at his ripe age – there was something the old herder could do. He could carry on with his walk, find his perfect spot, sit down and enjoy the view. And not even the might or madness of the German Army would stop him.

The two unlikely war machines landed several seconds apart from each other and Brooke had them rendezvous above a crossroads.

'I've brought us down a few clicks from the compound,' she said, taking the lead of a low-level push northwards. 'How are you finding the controls?'

'Tickety-boo,' said Jackson, rolling his vehicle erratically about its axes and leaving a *Tug*-sized hole in a wooden fence before tucking the robot in behind *Punk*.

'Both units are powered electrically, but *Tug* has an additional fuel cell which feeds a pulse jet. It can deliver a maximum of two shunts before all the fuel in the cell is exhausted.'

'Shunts?' asked Jackson.

Brooke realized that Jackson hadn't yet seen the robot he was controlling. He knew little more about it than the scant facts she had emailed for him to build the control mechanism.

'You're flying a space tug, the muscle in my father's vision for a roughneck gang of space miners. The idea is that ten or twenty tugs could attach themselves to valuable pieces of floating rock, then use powerful jet engines to shunt the rock into position so other members of the gang can extract cobalt, platinum, titanium and other valuable metals for haulin' back to Earth.'

'I'm guessing that's what the CLAW and MAGNET are for?' He'd mapped these functions on to his control device, at Brooke's request.

'Yessir.'

'And the GRENADE?' Jackson expected he'd like this explanation.

'Thermite. It was used by Special Forces soldiers in the Second World War against tanks. Dad wanted a crowd-pleaser for his investors. It's a mixture of powdered aluminium and iron oxide that burns at a very high temperature – over 2,500 degrees centigrade. That's hot enough to turn anything metal into liquid. It would be no good in space, a bit like *Punk*'s rotors, but perfect for our test site.'

'So what's your robot packing?'

'*Punk* is the boffin of the group. He's designed to gather information, film, photograph and perform tests on rock formations so the other bots know where to dig. You should see what he's giving me back now, almost 360 degrees of vision, thanks to twelve cameras all over his cute little body. *Punk* has a few tricks up his sleeve too, but I'm not intending to use them. It's important we keep a lid on things, Jackson – this mission is all about getting *Punk* into a position where he can gather the evidence we need to persuade Lear to give up the twins and hopefully close him down for good. I'm in enough trouble as it is . . . the last thing I need is an international incident to lay at Pops' door.'

As the machines arrived on the ridge above the compound where they had last been as part of MeX, Brooke and Jackson grew quiet. The shape of the valley, with its sheer bottleneck at one end, looked familiar, but everything else about the place had changed. Where the compound had been there was nothing but hard-baked mud. It was smooth, flat and clean – freakishly clean. From the base of the largest cliff to where the fence once stood, there wasn't even a tyre track or a single piece of discarded trash. In place of the buildings were just four dusted rectangles, like the footprints of a huge alien spaceship that had touched down and sucked up everything in sight. The clean-up didn't make it any less of a disaster area. For Jackson, there was something in this arid scene that foretold what would come if Lear's plans were left unchecked.

'There's nothin' left to photograph,' said Brooke despondently. As the two combed the valley floor with the mining bots, it became clear how clinical the clean-up operation had been. The base of the biggest mountains had undergone the most amazing transformation. The cavernous gash housing the water-pipe exchange had completely vanished, and in its place was smooth rock.

'Are you getting this?' asked Jackson, hovering *Tug* next to what appeared to be a massive plug made of rock. To anyone else, the huge bung in the rock wall would have been invisible, its edges perceived as natural cracks in the rock. But both roboteers had seen the close-up footage from Brooke's camera on their previous visit and knew this was the place where billions of litres of stolen water had terminated.

Jackson had a flashback to the patent website. 'It's a rock-plastic amalgam!' he declared. 'It was developed by Real Holdings.'

'A what?'

'It's similar to the stuff they use for making climbing walls. It's like rock, but it's not rock. They must have just squirted it in, like a dentist filling a cavity. It's very clever – by the time anyone discovers it, they're long gone.'

'All I know is it doesn't really matter,' said Brooke, sounding frustrated. 'There's nothing that will come out on film here. Unless we're looking to enter Lear for a Best Kept Valley Award, I reckon our best bet now is to head for the vanished village. We can only hope there's enough evidence left to link Lear to the devastation and persuade him to let the Kojimas go.'

'A few pictures of the crumbled foundations of a village no one's heard of won't be enough to make Lear or anyone else sit up and listen, Brooke. We need to get to the other side of the mountain. Lear is treating it like a bank. He deposits the water in one end and then draws it out of the other. And what's on the other side? Moldova!'

'Come off it . . . whatever that swindler was up to, he's long gone now.'

'D'you remember our research on the area for the original mission?' asked Jackson.

'Nope,' replied Brooke. 'I only read what I had to – I is here for the machines, remember!'

Jackson raised an eyebrow, invisible to Brooke on the other side of the world. 'Fine. Well, listen to this,' he said, minimizing his view from *Tug* to bring up a web page he had looked at for very different reasons a week ago.

> The former Soviet country of Moldova has a thriving black market, where all kinds of contraband are available. Anything from ex-Russian tanks to nuclear materials and oil are known to be trafficked across its border, using long-established smuggling routes and gangs.

'If there's a place where Lear could find a buyer for his water, it's there! Why settle for a few snaps of an ex-village when we can film his whole operation? That way, we'll have enough to secure the twins' release and end his operation for good!'

'All right. But whatever we do – it had better be quick.' As Brooke sent *Punk* after Jackson's stout machine, the banging and cries from the other side of the steel door were giving way to the sound of drilling.

J.P.'s voice had boomed loud in the speaker until Brooke turned it off, but she'd have to live with the drilling of the metal door. Her father had access to a real-time stream of data from the mission. He might not understand where his robotic prototypes had gone, but he knew they had taken a downward trajectory over the western edge of Russia – and that his daughter had locked the rest of the launch team out, to make it happen. She could see her furious father pacing up and down and gesticulating at the camera that fed the screen above her station.

T minus fifteen minutes till Pops gets in here, she thought.

CHAPTER 31

The land beyond the mountain top was a smear of purple black below a mackerel sky, as if the sun got to choose a new colour for each country. Jackson was using a combination of topographical information from his research and gut instinct that whatever Lear was up to on the other side of the mountain had to be within spitting distance of a road of some kind. There were three roads leading to the foot of the mountain on the Moldovan side – he led the robots down towards the one furthest from the official border crossing.

Punk's sensitive microphones picked up the soft crump of explosions first, and then the faint echo of rifle fire. And it wasn't long before Brooke and Jackson could make out the telltale shapes of Lear's road-trains, like big black grubs lining up to feed. They pulled the two robots close to the edge of a large rocky horseshoe where they couldn't be spotted.

'OK, Factoid Boy, what are they up to down there?'

'I'm not entirely sure, but it makes sense that the Moldovan dealers will use their black-market connections to find the highest bidder for Lear's water. It's as valuable as oil. In some countries, where there are huge water shortages, they refer to it as "liquid gold". There is either not enough to go round, or it's polluted or controlled by rogue governments. The government of Bolivia, for example, sold the rights to all their natural water to a corporation. If you collected a cupful of rainwater in a downpour, you'd have to pay to drink it! If they can't get the price they want locally, they'll just send it elsewhere.'

'How d'you find that stuff out? Do you ever sleep?'

'Yeah, well, someone I know went and got themselves kidnapped in a different time zone – and I've been jet-lagged ever since.'

'OK, so Lear has the makings of another very profitable business – as if he needs it – but how's it work here?'

'I'm guessing the Moldovan gang are the couriers. They find a buyer and send it on.'

'Sure, but how do you *send* billions of litres of water?'

'In the same way as oil . . . you use pipes and boats!'

The summer in this part of Eastern Europe was just beginning, but the days were hot enough, and the nights cool enough, to mix up a thin fog that shrouded the two robots as they descended to a vantage point above the action. There had been the odd snap of gunfire, but nothing like the thuds and rumbles that had brought them here. As *Punk* offered Brooke a full panorama of the one-time wasteland, now converted into a busy hub for big rigs, pick-ups and armed guards, she became aware of some strange flashes from inside the trees across the valley.

'You won't believe this,' said Brooke, who had zoomed in on the tree line with one of *Punk*'s telescopic lenses.

'Don't tell me,' replied Jackson. 'Dragos.'

The General, with a mixture of his militiamen and ten or so shabby-looking civilians who doubtless had followed him from the vanished village, were holed up above the compound. Brooke panned her view further down the slope and recognized the army-green jump-suits of a few groups of Lear's security men. It looked like two squads of Lear's men were making their way up to Dragos's position. The two groups of fighters were about a hundred metres or so apart – an advance party, whom Brooke assumed were tasked with flushing out the General, and a rearguard to finish him and his men off.

'I'm no expert,' said Brooke. 'But by the looks of the load-out Lear's men are carrying, our handsome General is outgunned.' The auto-focus on *Punk*'s camera was moving between the shiny faces of Lear's men and the assortment of scary-looking weapons on their backs.

'Do you know what really bugs me?' said Jackson. 'The fact that Lear isn't down there himself.' But even as he said it he suspected that Lear was there in all but body – like a poltergeist, watching, listening and keeping things moving.

'He doesn't need to be,' said Brooke. 'If you can get all this on camera, the only water supply he'll be getting his hands on will be the sink in his jail cell. We better get on with this. You could try getting *Tug* in between Dragos and the advancing soldiers.'

'What's *Tug* going to do – shunt Lear's heavies into submission?'

'No, we don't want to get into a fight we can't win. I dunno . . . create a diversion, while me and *Punk* get busy with our photo shoot.'

Jackson dipped his control stick forward. He had J. P.'s computer-assisted fly-by-wire system to thank for the ease of handling. All he had to do was watch that he didn't pitch the nose too steeply – get the balance wrong and, as he'd found during the earlier part of their journey, *Tug* would bite the dirt, digging up great chunks of earth. Do that here, where there was little else but rock and pine trees, and Jackson could say goodbye to his robot.

Jackson aimed for the rearguard first, a tight formation of just four men. *Tug*'s electric fan screamed just millimetres above their heads, sending the men scurrying for cover like silverfish. It took the men only a few seconds to come to their senses, and a hail of gunfire followed *Tug*. Jackson seized his chance and pulled back on his chrome metal stick to flip the robot on to his back, then dropped him behind a row of bushes. To the rearguard whose bullets were chasing him, it looked like whatever had just buzzed them had been downed, and they set off, weapons primed, to investigate.

Tug had left the unit looking for him in the stunted shrubs that clung to the hillside and now circled around the vanguard group, using wispy pockets of fog for cover. But, as he approached Lear's men, Jackson spotted a new threat to Dragos and his band of freedom fighters in the corner of *Tug*'s video feed. A battered Land Rover with a large-calibre machine gun mounted in the back was picking a route up the hillside. Jackson reckoned the Ukrainians had about a minute before the long-haired brute behind the machine gun zeroed in on them.

Throwing *Tug* across the slope towards the vehicle, he had the robot break cover fifty metres from the converted off-roader. As *Tug* approached at speed, Jackson could clearly see the Land Rover's driver shouting to the man behind him to open fire. Without really knowing what to expect, Jackson depressed the button on his lightsabre handle, which he'd mapped to the CLAW function. Seconds from impact and *Tug*'s nose opened, splitting into two sections of a powerful pincer. The gunner's enraged face lit up as he pulled the trigger, and several rounds of burning red tracer flew either side of Jackson's view before his robot butted the gun barrel.

As soon as they impacted the gun, *Tug*'s pincers closed round it, ripping the weapon from its housing and knocking the gunner off his feet. Jackson released *Tug*'s grip and the mangled weapon clattered on to the rocks, then he brought him into a steady hover in front of the Land Rover.

The driver sat open-mouthed, the fear in his eyes showing through his cracked windscreen. And *Tug*'s optics were sensitive enough for Jackson to notice the driver's eyes suddenly focus as he understood the consequences of the robot's next move.

In all honesty, Jackson was a little disappointed at what happened when he pressed his GRENADE button. A small canister, about the size of a fizzy drinks can and covered in a treacly, gloppy substance, shot from the robot and stuck to the vehicle's hood. For a good ten seconds nothing happened. The driver just stared into *Tug*'s camera, and Jackson stared into his monitor back at him. Then the grenade started to fizz and smoke and a brilliant plume of molten metal and sparks spurted into the air. When his engine stopped, the driver knew whatever was in the can had made it to his engine, and he wasn't staying to find out if it could eat the rest of his car.

Brooke had heard the firing up on the hillside, but she was too focused on her side of the mission to worry. *Punk* was hovering beside the cabin of one of Lear's massive rigs. Of all the views offered up, the one that interested the young American most was showing her a portable office building in which she could just make out four men chatting. Doing her best to keep an eye on all eight of *Punk*'s camera feeds, she sent the robot towards the mobile office, bringing him to rest on the building's roof. After retracting the rotorblades, *Punk* rolled slowly forward and a few degrees to the right, until his listening spike was touching the thin flat roof of the movable building.

It took a moment for Brooke to tune her ears into the thick East European accent of one of the men. He spoke in a monotone with a measured voice and his 'r's were rolled.

'How long until your pipeline is ready to connect to ours?'

'The first of our trucks have already reached the outskirts of Giurgiulesti.' The second voice belonged to an Englishman, or a European who spoke very good English. It was precise and businesslike, with no hint of colour; the voice of a military man, she thought. 'I anticipate we should be able to start pumping within the next thirty minutes, Mr Josan. Assuming you have greased the right palms?'

'Everything will go smoothly at our end,' said the East European. 'You can tell your boss that if this first transaction is successful, my network stands ready to connect you and your . . . product to markets who will pay more for it than oil.'

'Believe me, sir, once we have completed certain operations we have planned for the water supplies of vulnerable nations, our *product* will be worth more than gold! We have found that a little poison, or even the rumour of contamination, has made the water we offer extremely desirable.'

If Brooke understood what the man in the cabin had just said, Lear, the supposed 'friendly face of computing', was about to add the wholesale poisoning of water to the theft, kidnapping and murder he was already responsible for. Thankfully, she had it all recorded. And now, as the four men dropped from the cabin on to the grass, she had their faces too.

'Does "Giurgiulesti" mean anything to you?' said Brooke, her voice crackling in Jackson's headphones.

'Of course. It's Moldova's only port. Privately owned and operated. It's connected to the sea by the lower Danube river.'

'Well, that's where they're sending the water.'

'What did I tell you – he's using boats!'

It made complete sense. Using huge tankers, the water could be shipped to whoever in the world was willing to pay the highest price. Jackson had seen huge tankers on the Web that carried what were called Bulk Liquid Cargoes. Every day, oil, liquid gas, chemicals, even wine, were carried across thousands of miles of ocean. *Imagine that*, he'd thought. *A wine slick!* Lear's liquid cargo wasn't any different. The predictions of global water shortages that he'd read about would only make Lear's watery ambitions much more profitable.

The drilling had stopped. All Brooke could hear now were the grunts and curses of Goulman, applying his body builder's physique to the end of a crowbar in order to peel back the edges of the door.

'Jackson, I reckon we got about five minutes before my dad gatecrashes his own party. Am I hearin' things or are you startin' a brawl up there?'

'You just keep snapping,' Jackson replied, watching the Land Rover's front tyres blow out as molten engine metal congealed round them. 'Me and *Tug* have things under control.'

Jackson wasn't entirely convinced if his confidence was well placed as he turned *Tug* round and looked back up the hillside. While he had been dealing with the Land Rover, Dragos and his men had engaged the security men that formed the rearguard. Their shabby appearance belied amazing skill and, after a brief but fearsome fire-fight, Lear's men gave up and joined the Land Rover driver in running away down the hillside. But as *Tug* got closer, Jackson could see that Lear's other mercenary unit was now on the offensive, raining down a storm of automatic gunfire on the General's position.

Jackson could see that several of Dragos's fighters had been injured and some members of the team were carrying them off in a bid to retreat, while the General attempted to cover them. *Tug* banked hard above the rocky outcrop on which the remaining gaggle of Dragos's men were marooned. Jackson could see the brave General with his signature black beret and the four remaining villagers at his side, attempting to hold back at least ten heavily armed mercenaries. But for each shot they fired, they received a barrage in return.

Jackson knew it was only a matter of minutes before they were overrun. He tilted *Tug* into a steep dive, pulling up so close to the hillside that clumps of dry grass lashed at the edges of his view. Then he flung the robot sideways, so his back was to Dragos and his nose was trained on Lear's unit, and began to circle them. He was 'slicing the pie', a gaming tactic he'd used to devastating effect in countless virtual battles. The idea was to force your enemy to turn on the spot, preventing them from setting up a steady aim. It was no different here, with the sideways-moving robot sweeping a speedy arc round the hired shooters, causing them to empty their maga-zines with wayward shots as each of them attempted to pirouette and keep the flying machine in their sights.

As the shooting dried up, Jackson pushed *Tug* towards the men while pressing his thumb over the tiny metal knob to which he'd assigned the MAGNET function. The effect was instant. Some of the men squealed as their fingers were twisted and their metal weapons were wrenched from their hands. Jackson had to apply extra thrust just to keep *Tug* from dropping like a stone with the extra weight of the rifles and machine guns now stuck all over his underside. Without warning, Dragos and his four men leaped from the rocks and ran into the midst of the disarmed unit.

It was hard for Jackson to see the details of the fight, given that the curved magazine of an AK47 assault rifle was covering *Tug*'s camera lens. But it was less than a minute before half of Lear's unit were cowering at the feet of Dragos's biggest man – an enormous villager who, but for his large blue lumberjack shirt, could have been mistaken for a very angry bear – while the other half were being pursued up the mountain.

Jackson had just released the MAGNET function, letting the weapons drop to the ground, when *Tug* was suddenly hit by something, as if the robot had been slapped by a giant hockey stick. All Jackson could see was ground and sky in lightning quick rotation, until

Tug slammed into the floor of the compound, finishing upside down at the foot of the slope, a smouldering stump where the tip of his left wing should have been.

J.P. and Goulman had bent back so much metal, they almost had an arm in the operations room. Brooke quickly captured the insides of one of the pipe-laying road-trains that was coupled up to a large chrome tap-exchange at the base of the mountain, ready to file-transfer to a secure server at her dad's ranch with the other photos and video. She positioned *Punk* for a final shot of what she guessed was a massive drilling machine, badly hidden under ill-fitting tarpaulin on the back of an eighteen-wheeler, when her MeX handset rang.

CHAPTER 32

'Hello, Farley,' Lear said, as Jackson warily connected to the MeX handset, which he had never expected to ring again. 'My, how you've let your standards slide. And where exactly did you get hold of that piece of farmyard machinery you're driving? I'm sorry, *were* driving. Don't tell me . . . it's one of J.P.'s inventions. I guess I should be impressed that you both made it here. Miss English, does your esteemed father know you have borrowed his flying trash cans?'

'Bite me!' replied Brooke, furious that *Punk* had now joined *Tug* and was lying greasy side up at the edge of the compound.

'Rotor blades!' said Lear. 'How quaint! And what about those spikes? Do they do anything, or are they merely for effect?'

'Why don't you reveal yourself and I can show you!' the young American shot back through clenched teeth.

A glassy disc appeared in front of one of Lear's big

rigs, the outline of a MeX saucer, but with a shimmering crystalline skin in place of the slate-grey of the MEX$_1$s that Brooke and Jackson had piloted. It was easy to see how the Cloaker worked as the image of the truck's black tyres and chrome hubcaps slowly faded from the smooth skin on which they had been synthesized. It wasn't so much invisibility as blending in. Now that Jackson knew where it was hovering, it would no longer be able to blend in quite so effectively, like a picture of a stick insect after someone has pointed out that one of the sticks has legs. Jackson could also make out the mouth of a gun barrel, which he knew had launched the projectile that had downed *Tug*.

'Big deal! So you strapped a TV to the outside of one of your flying soup bowls,' said Brooke nonchalantly. 'But you won't be *invisible* to the authorities once we release the evidence we've gathered. Of course, you could make it easier on yourself by telling us where you've hidden the twins.'

'You'll find out soon enough,' Lear replied.

'What I don't understand is why,' Brooke continued. 'Aren't you rich enough?'

'*To dare is to do.*' Lear sighed heavily. 'Oh, come now – is what we're doing here so different from what our governments are doing with oil, with gold, with diamonds? It's endearing that the two of you see things so simply – as either *good* or *evil*. But really . . . when you both get a little older you'll understand – there are two sides to everything.'

'Tell that to Mr Mobius,' said Jackson. It was a phrase his mother used to say. It referred to the Mobius Strip, a simple band of paper given a twist and then joined at its ends. It was a mathematical peculiarity and, in Jackson's mind at least, proof that something that appears to be two-sided can also be one-sided.

'Ideological and a maths bore – what an unfortunate combination,' sneered Lear.

'Try evil and slightly balding,' Brooke quipped.

Devlin Lear was silent, failing to hide his embarrass-ment at being trumped.

'You'll forgive me if I don't chat. As you've noticed, I am a little busy right now. So, if you don't want to witness Dragos and his hardy band of hangers-on blown to smithereens by my Cloaker's bullets, I suggest you give me exclusive access to whatever server you've stored all your surveillance data on. Thirty seconds should give you enough time to send me the login details – but not long enough for you to copy the files – if you get my drift.'

'And what makes you think we'll just roll over?' Jackson wasn't entirely sure how his argument came across, given his machine was lying on its back with part of its wing missing.

'Perhaps this will help persuade you . . .' Two more

Cloakers revealed themselves, hovering a metre or so above the ground on either side of Lear's MeX$_3$.

'Say hello to the twins! They've been helping me to keep an eye on you ever since I was informed of your arrival.'

Jackson was gutted. He couldn't believe what Lear was telling him. He'd spent so many days and nights worrying about the fate of his ex-teammates, only to be faced with this. Was it really them?

Brooke was apparently convinced. 'Tell them from me they're owned!' she spat.

'Oh, they can hear you . . . they just choose to ignore you,' said Lear.

The two glistening discs hung in the air with the Kojimas' distinctive stacked formation – one on top of the other. As they moved slowly off towards the mountainside, their luminous skins morphed into shimmering outlines before vanishing altogether against the dark escarpment.

Jackson recognized the twins' machines by their distinctive flying style and knew it was all over. He didn't need to question Brooke – he knew she'd give up the files rather than see the General and his men slaughtered. *She's right*, he told himself. *Dragos will die. Lear will worm his way out. We are no match for this man. We never were.* He shook his head to force out the fearful thoughts, and they were immediately replaced with something else. The voice of Willard from the chess club. *I know you can think, Farley – the question is, can you fight?*

He wanted to fight, but this man was a cold-blooded murderer.

'Nothing to say?' sneered Lear. 'What is it exactly you need to prove, Farley? Do you really think you'll ever climb as high as that pedestal you put your dead mother on?'

Lear's words startled Jackson. What did he mean by bringing his mother into it? He'd shown he had access to information about the recruits, Jackson even imagined he'd revelled in spying on them, but this was low even for Lear.

'You know nothing about my mother!' snarled Jackson. At the same moment, he let his index finger slide on to the metal bead at the top of the lightsabre that sat heavy in his hand. No sooner had Jackson engaged the SHUNT, than *Tug* shot forward. Still upended, the robot scraped across the ground, sparks arcing from the metal edges of his fuselage as he rocketed towards Lear's machine. Before Lear had time to react, *Tug* had collided with his MeX$_3$, flipping it up and over the juggernaut like a huge coin.

'What are you doing?' yelled Brooke.

'Just follow me. We have to head off the twins before they reach Dragos.'

Tug tore away, Jackson flipping the robot right side

up and compensating for the missing wing tip by holding his controller at a right angle. Brooke wavered for a beat. Jackson's decision had taken her by surprise. It was fool-hardy and potentially lethal for the men on the hill. The imminent arrival of her father through the door and the fact that both her robots were perilously low on power had weakened her resolve. But she loathed the fact that Lear had outfoxed them. What was all this for if Lear's crimes didn't end up being laid bare? Brooke snapped her joystick forward and committed *Punk* to the chase.

'How we gonna *head off* something we can't see?' It was a stumbling block all right. They were chasing two of the most advanced dot.robots, built for the fight. The Kojimas hopelessly outgunned them and Brooke suspected there was a good chance Lear's machine would soon be joining the fray.

'Just keep on *Tug*'s tail,' said Jackson. 'I've think I know how to uncloak them!'

Tug's handling had been seriously impaired by the MeX$_3$'s explosive bullet, and the robot whipsawed from side to side as he joined *Punk* to crest the ridge a few hundred metres below the General's position. All that stood between them and Dragos was the thin coating of mist, which had thickened since their arrival. The screens of both pilots whited out for a few seconds as *Tug* and *Punk* disappeared inside the fog band that surrounded the mountain. Jackson was relieved to see Dragos and his companions lowering their guns when they recognized the outline of his damaged machine as the one that had helped them earlier. Their reaction to *Punk* was less welcoming, but something about the slipshod spiked ball told the villagers this wasn't one of Lear's creations.

'Keep your eyes on the fog,' Jackson warned Brooke. 'They'll have seen us on their spider displays and they'll be coming.' The rudimentary navigation display that J.P. had given his two mining bots was designed for nothing more testing than their Mojave demonstration. They had no infrared, and their radar was designed to give a simple outline of the terrain so they could locate or avoid large rock formations. Jackson knew from experience that the MeX craft had a full spectrum of navigation and object-detection systems at their disposal; if nothing else, they would have caught their heat signals as they'd passed through the mist.

Jackson put his face close to the monitor, searching for a sign in the ghostly fog. Then he noticed a break in the milky wall, as if someone had cut out a porthole in the cloud of water vapour. The Cloaker was doing its job, mimicking the dense white cloud that its panoramic camera saw all around it – but its intricate electronics couldn't account for the fact that the saucer-shaped object had cut a path through the fog.

Jackson fired his thruster for the final time and *Tug*'s potent fuel cell drained the last dregs of energy into the engine. The robot surged forward so quickly that he corkscrewed around his roll axis. *Tug*'s chisel-shaped nose struck the MeX_3 with enough force to crack open its thermoplastic casing and send it rolling down the hillside. The force also caused *Tug* to somersault on to the ground, digging himself a rut in the soft soil. Suddenly the second of the twins' machines punctured the fog. *Punk* shot towards the disc-shaped apparition, his rotor-blades retracting just before his metal body hit the MeX_3 like a spiked wrecking ball. Several of the little robot's sharp metal spikes pierced the plastic airframe of the Cloaker and Brooke engaged what she affectionately called *Punk*'s cattle prod. It wasn't a prod as such, but a means of sending a high-voltage electric charge through all of *Punk*'s sharp spines at once. The Kojimas' machine was consumed in a blinding blue-and-white flash that lit up the edges of the fog. The defeated dot. robot dropped lifelessly to the ground, with *Punk* still attached.

'And that's what you call a slam-dunk!' shouted Brooke triumphantly.

For a moment Jackson felt numb. Had it been that easy? He opened his mouth to speak to Brooke when suddenly *Tug* was snatched away by what seemed like a mighty gust of wind. One moment the two asteroid-mining machines were hovering before Dragos and their comrades in arms, the next they were dashed against the rocks behind. As Dragos and his men dived for cover, a familiar shape loomed out of the mist. It was Lear's MeX_3, uncloaked and spitting sparks from its ruptured Optical Skin, but flying straight and steady. And it was clear from the effects of the Bass Bomb that had just hit *Tug* and *Punk* that its weapons were functioning perfectly.

'Login details ... Now!' the Englishman's voice boomed. An intense greenish-blue light erupted from the centre of Lear's machine. It made Jackson wince and look away from his screen. His eyeballs felt like they'd been flash-fried. But his discomfort was little compared to the men whose cries he could hear all around him.

'The next dose from my Dazzler will blind them permanently. Login details. Now!'

'OK ... OK ...' said Brooke.

Tug was beaten. Jackson could see his robot's battery indicator had bottomed out and when he tried to move the battered robot, the electric fan let out a sickly splutter. There was a large crack across the centre of the sideways view that the broken machine was offering Jackson, but the video feed was clear enough for him to make out the two machines controlled by the Kojimas coming into view through the fog. Even if *Punk* had another round left in him, Jackson knew the fight was over.

'The username is "scumbag" . . . I kinda named that one after you,' said Brooke. As she spoke, Jackson was amazed to see the two machines piloted by the twins arriving either side of Lear's. After everything he and Brooke had thrown at the twins' MeX$_3$s, they were battered but clearly still functioning.

'And the password . . .' Brooke was about to hand over the final key to all that they had on the maniacal billionaire when the two machines flanking him suddenly exploded. In a fraction of a second the twins' machines were incinerated and Lear's was engulfed in flames.

Brooke was so amazed at what her screen was showing that she failed to notice the figures of her father, his breathless assistant and the elfin launch director standing behind her, the door having finally succumbed to their assault.

'Two birds . . . one stone.' It was the voice of Master Kojima.

'I don't understand . . .' said Brooke into the MeX handset through which she'd just heard his voice. But before she could finish her sentence, the line went dead.

'I guess MeX is offline! I think the great Devlin Lear just ran out of things to say,' said Jackson.

No one said a word. Not J.P., his baffled colleagues or the two roboteers, as they stared into the monitors watching the five warriors gather one by one round the burning shell of Lear's Cloaker. Dragos fired one round from a pistol into the flames and his men followed suit, emptying their weapons into the fiery remains and then beating the ground with their rifle butts. And in the flames and the silhouettes that seemed to dance around them like ancient warriors, there was something majestic and meaningful.

CHAPTER 33

It was raining, again. Jackson could see a globule of water forming on his window sill, feeding a tiny stream that flowed along a crack in the paintwork that sent rhythmic drips into his waste-paper basket, so each splat sounded like the tick of a clock. *How can I adjust the flow of water from the gap in my window so that the interval between 'ticks' is precisely one second?* Short of building his own Cloudbuster, an actual invention he'd read about that claimed to offer its user the ability to control clouds, Jackson couldn't see how his 'rain-clock' equation would work. In any case, he probably wouldn't see the calculations through. He'd found it hard to focus on anything in the week or so since the 'Moldovan Hoedown' as his American friend kept referring to it.

They had spoken to the Kojimas. Lear had made them believe that Jackson and Brooke had both left MeX – that after seeing the Ukrainian villagers, they'd decided they couldn't do it any more. The twins had known nothing of the information Jackson had uncovered or of Brooke's kidnapping and were still waiting for the next mission that Miss Kojima had so wistfully asked about when they were last together. When they'd realized what was happening during the last mission, they had instantly decided to trust their old teammates and had emerged through the fog in an attempt to signal their alliance.

Brooke and Jackson laughed as they recalled the beating *Tug* and *Punk* had dished out to the twins' machines, when all they'd been trying to do was join forces – *Punk* springing on to the robot twice his size and *Tug* bringing down a superior piece of technology with his own brand of headbutt. Still, the actions of the Japanese brother and sister had confirmed Jackson's belief that he had three loyal and brilliant friends, despite the whole MeX disaster.

He wanted to return to his old life as if nothing had changed. But the list of things that had seemed so important before – chess club, Tyler Hughes, *Whisper* – felt somehow trivial. Lear had been right about one thing – MeX had filled a gap in his life. And thoughts of the billionaire still haunted Jackson. He shivered uncomfortably. Lear was wrong. Jackson wasn't like him. *He wasn't.*

OK, strike Whisper *from that list*, he told himself. His computer was already on and he fired up the game. WizardZombie was curled up beside the cinders of his campfire. Jackson directed him to stand and he dutifully picked up his longbow and slung a cloth pouch over his back. Jackson let his character stand a while and the two of them took in a beautiful sunset.

They were ready for their next adventure.

●CHAPTER 34

The bistro owed a debt of gratitude to the private hospital that had recently been constructed across the street. Where once the Paraguayan afternoon sun was hot enough to cook the salads they served on their terrace, the arrival of the tallest building in this part of town had cast a broad shadow over just about all of their outdoor tables. They'd been fully booked ever since.

A waiter had just seated a customer he'd come to refer to as 'El Capitan'. The smart-looking gentleman had arrived at the restaurant several days ago and after the keen young waiter had served him several courses he politely asked what he did for a living. The man, who was dressed in an immaculate white linen suit, red polka-dot cravat and panama hat, had answered in perfect Spanish, with only the tiniest hint of an English accent. 'What do *you* think I do for a living?'

The young man had thought for a moment and said, in his native tongue, 'I believe you are a sailor. The captain of a tall ship!'

'You are not wrong,' the smart man had said. And indeed he did own a rather impressive yacht, which was moored about five kilometres along the coast.

The waiter liked El Capitan. He wasn't ignorant like most foreigners. He spoke the language and he gave the most generous tips he'd ever received. And anyway, he felt sorry for him. He wanted to know what terrible accident must have befallen him, that both his hands should be bandaged and his face too. He imagined that he might have an allergy to the sun, or have been slashed by one of the machete-wielding pirate gangs that in recent years had hung around the ports like bacterial cultures. But he had decided it would be impolite to ask.

The smart man found the heat of the sun made the skin under his bandages itch. But then it itched like mad anyway, especially near his ears where the roughest of his stitches were, and on his fingertips where the skin had been taken off. There was no way round it – getting a new identity was a painful process.

It was bright enough for him to read his newspaper without taking off his sunglasses. He studied the headline story on the front of *The Paraguay Post*.

LEAR FEARED DEAD

Coastguards are giving up their search for Internet pioneer Devlin Lear whose yacht disappeared in a storm earlier this week. Billionaire Lear is believed to have a fleet of several luxurious floating homes anchored around the world. Friends and colleagues have expressed surprise that the experienced sailor got into trouble in what the local weather service described as 'moderate storm conditions'. In a further twist to the story, Mr Lear is wanted for questioning over video and phone recordings that point to his involvement in shady water rights dealings in Eastern Europe. Videos and photographs of alleged illicit activities involving 'the friendly face of computing', as he has become known, have been appearing on websites, posted by an anonymous source. Lear Corporation legal teams have been attempting to embargo the uploads, but so far have been unable to prevent the material from appearing on the Internet.

The smart man took a bright white handkerchief from inside the pocket of his blazer and used it to delicately mop up a line of sweat that had formed between the edge of the bandage on his forehead and the thin wisps of blond hair.

He then finished his coffee, placed a twenty-dollar bill underneath a glass on the table and stood up.

There was a plastic bin loosely attached by wire to the stem of a street lamp and, as he crossed the pavement, the smart man threw the folded newspaper at it. Remarkably, he missed and the paper landed on the road. The smart man felt a slight tingle of pleasure when he placed his brown leather brogue squarely on the story he had just read, as he made his way across the empty street.

●ACKNOWLEDGEMENTS

Book writing seems, from the outside at least, like a lonely business. In reality, it's a team effort. The *Dot. Robot* team consists of oodles of strangers who listened and smiled politely as I enthused on trains and in cafes. It also includes my teachers, who all (and I do mean *all*) inspired in me a love of words and numbers. And then there's each of my beta testers – my buddies Rich and Jamie, the boy at the end of my road, Joss, and my nephew Jacob who speaks Messenger language better than anyone.

My heartfelt thanks go to my TV agent, Debbie, and my literary agent, Luigi Bonomi, who were the first professional types to take my idea for a twelve-year-old computer-gaming roboteer-maths-genius seriously.

I must also thank *The Gadget Show* team, Ewan Keil in particular, for opening up a trove of technological treasure and paying me to play with it.

I'll never forget the day that Puffin Books said 'Yes!' to *Dot.Robot*. If the Puffin gang's energy and enthusiasm for children's books could be bottled, there would be no need for oil. And a special thanks to my editor, Lindsey Heaven, who has a doctor's handwriting but a surgeon's skill – and who I count as my newest friend.

I have read many great books while dreaming up and fact-checking *Dot.Robot*, but the one I would recommend to anyone with an interest in space and science is *A Tribble's Guide to Space*. Thanks to Alan C. Tribble's amazing book, the space stuff in *Dot.Robot* should be spot on.

Finally, I must acknowledge my long-suffering girlfriend, Claire, without whose patience and support none of my words would have made it to the page.

How do you follow that?
Easy with more . . .

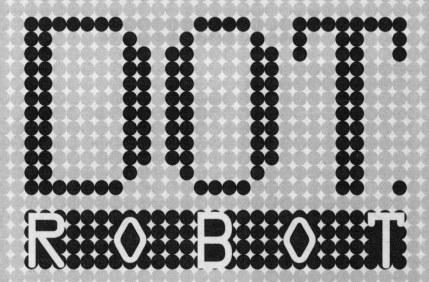

D.O.T.
ROBOT

THE NEXT
INSTALMENT
COMING FEBRUARY 2010

Crack the code and enter the hidden MeX network

INTRUSION DETECTION:
ON

FIREWALL SETTINGS:
HIGH

ANTI-VIRUS:
MEDIUM

TOP

YOU WILL BE CONTACTED AGAIN SOON . . .

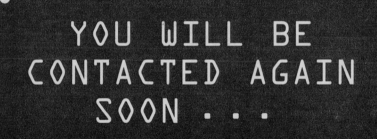

NEED YOU NOW!
Launch the MeX training simulator
Have your Dazzlers ready for an ultra-addictive deathmatch
SECRET
ACCESS ALL AREAS
at doyouknowanysecrets.com